OMEGA PLACE

Also by Graham Marks

Radio Radio

How It Works

Zoo

Tokyo

OMEGA PLACE

GOING UNDERGROUND . . .

Graham Marks

BLOOMSBURY

Acknowledgements

Big thanks to Gregory Wells, for taking the time to plough through an early iteration (and liking it), Eileen Armstrong for her valuable comments, and my editors, Isabel Ford and Georgia Murray, for their clarity of vision. Sometimes – make that often – you can't see the book for the words.

First published in Great Britain in 2007 by Bloomsbury Publishing Plc
36 Soho Square, London, W1D 3QY

Copyright © Graham Marks 2007
The moral right of the author has been asserted

A CIP catalogue record of this book is available from the British Library

ISBN 978 0 7475 8963 1

All papers used by Bloomsbury Publishing are natural, recyclable products made
from wood grown in well-managed forests. The manufacturing processes conform
to the environmental regulations of the country of origin.

Typeset by Dorchester Typesetting Group Ltd
Printed in Great Britain by Clays Ltd, St Ives Plc

1 3 5 7 9 10 8 6 4 2

www.bloomsbury.com
www.marksworks.co.uk

*This is for my Ma, who lit the flame of story in my head,
and for Maggie Noach, who kept it burning bright.
Goodbye to both of you.*

For some must watch, while some must sleep.
      Thus runs the world away.
                              William Shakespeare, Hamlet (1600)

Quis custodiet ipsos custodies?
(Who watches the watchmen?)
                              Decimus Junius Juvenalis (1st century AD)

1

Monday 21st August, Gosforth, Newcastle Upon Tyne

The doorbell *bing-bonged* in the hallway as Sandra Tennant was about to pour boiling water into the two coffee mugs on the work surface. Her husband, Mike, looked up from the paper, glanced at his watch – 5:50 p.m. – and frowned as he started to get up.

'Wonder who that can be at this time?'

'Well, it's not the postman, is it?' Sandra put the cordless kettle back down on its stand. 'Don't worry, love, I'll go . . .'

Through the open kitchen door, down at the end of the hall, she could see what looked like two figures, men, through the reeded glass. For a second she'd thought – hoped – It might be Paul. That he'd finally decided to come back home. But she could see it wasn't him as these people were wearing suits, and it occurred to her that it was probably Jehovah's Witnesses or Mormons. Someone selling something she didn't want, that was for sure. Getting to the end of the hallway she twisted the Yale lock and opened the door.

'Mrs Tennant?'

Sandra nodded, looking at the two men, one standing slightly behind the other. The boss and his assistant. Funny how you could always tell. She noticed their car, a dark blue Vauxhall saloon, parked in the drive; not the religious nuts, then, they always seemed to walk everywhere.

'Yes . . . What can I do for you?'

'My name's Detective Sergeant Maynard.' The man briefly held up and flipped open what looked like a black credit card holder. 'And this is Detective Constable Chambers. May we come in?'

'Who is it, Sandra?' Mike called from the kitchen.

'It's . . . it's the police, Mike . . .'

The atmosphere in the front room was one of anxious, almost fearful anticipation. As the two police officers had walked into the house, Sandra leading them down the hall, she could tell they'd brought bad news. It came in with them, along with the smell of stale cigarette smoke.

She'd immediately gone into delay mode, insisting on making the two men tea and leaving Mike to sit, uncomfortably, with them while she was in the kitchen. And now the tray – cups, saucers, side plates, teapot, sugar bowl, milk jug, biscuits and spoons – was on the table and she was sitting next to Mike. Nothing left to do. Time for the axe to fall.

DS Maynard looked at the biscuits but didn't take one. 'Is your son called Paul Hendry, Mrs Tennant?'

'Yes, yes he is . . .' Sandra looked at Mike. 'He never changed his name when I, when *we* got married.'

'Is something wrong, officer?' Mike took Sandra's hand.

'How long has he been missing?' DS Maynard appeared to be directing the question to both Mike and Sandra.

Sandra took a deep breath. 'Four . . . five weeks?'

'Why didn't you report it, Mrs Tennant?'

Sandra, chewing her lip, looked at the silent detective constable, who appeared to be making notes of everything that was said.

10

'Mrs Tennant?'

Mike shrugged. 'Look, officer, we thought he . . . we thought Paul was staying with friends, or maybe his dad.'

DS Maynard picked up the cup of tea Sandra had poured for him and took a sip. 'You didn't check?'

'It's been, I don't know, things have been . . . you know, *difficult*, haven't they, Sandra?' Sandra, staring at the floor, nodded slightly. 'I've tried, but we just don't get on. And he's a teenager, seventeen and some, but still a teenager, and you must know how they can be, officer: rows, unreasonable behaviour, acting like the world revolves around them . . . After the last shouting match he walked out with his rucksack. Broke the glass in the back door slamming it.'

'Why are you here, Detective Sergeant?' Sandra's voice was hushed, but had a distinct 'cut the crap' tone to it.

DS Maynard put his cup and saucer down. 'There's been an . . . incident . . . in London. And the information we've received, Mrs Tennant, indicates that it's possible your son has died.'

The words hung in the air like dust motes.

They made so little sense it was almost as if they'd been spoken in a foreign language. Sandra felt the breath sigh out of her and she thought for a moment that she was going to faint. Mike, picking up what might happen, moved closer to her and put an arm round her shoulder as she felt her eyes fill with tears.

Sandra shivered, even though it wasn't cold, and hugged herself, the words 'it's possible your son has died' echoing in the distance as the tears spilled down her cheeks.

'London? What was he doing in London, for Pete's sake?'

'We don't know for sure, Mrs Tennant. We were only

contacted last night, and I'm sorry, but we don't have very many details.'

'He's *dead*?' Sandra whispered.

Mike patted her shoulder as he gave her a couple of serviettes, the nearest thing to a tissue within easy reach. 'He just went, officer, never called us or anything . . .'

'Um . . .'

Silence. All heads turned to look at Sandra.

'I, um . . .' Sandra blew her nose. 'I had a text. You know, just saying he was OK?'

'Why didn't you say, love? Why didn't you tell me?'

There was no reply and the room fell silent again, this time for longer than was comfortable, no one knowing quite where to look; certainly not at this woman, trying to deal with the unthinkable. Then DC Chambers coughed and began checking back through his notes.

Sandra hugged herself tighter. 'I thought, you know, he'd be home any time . . .' She looked across at the senior of the two policemen. 'Are you *sure* he's dead, that it's him?'

DS Maynard turned, making a 'give it to me' gesture at DC Chambers, who handed over a buff-coloured A4 envelope. Opening it, the detective sergeant took out two inkjet colour prints and put them side by side on the table facing Sandra and Mike. One showed a close-up of a silver ring with a distinctive Celtic design, the other a small, gold shark's tooth on a gold chain.

'Do they belong to Paul, Mrs Tennant?'

Sandra Tennant nodded silently, collapsing against her husband.

DC Chambers backed the dark blue, unmarked Vectra out into the road, braked, and flicked the gear stick down, across and up into first. But instead of driving off he waited for a moment, looking back at the house, with its neat garden and trimmed hedges. In the sitting-room window he thought he could make out a figure looking back out at him.

'Doesn't seem like such a bad place to come from.'

'True.'

DC Chambers accelerated away. 'Didn't think the stepdad gave much of a shit.'

'Probably right there.'

'Maybe we should get him to do the ID, when the body comes up.'

'Maybe we should.'

'Why'd you just show them the two pictures, then?'

DS Maynard opened the buff envelope and pulled out a couple more prints of the scene-of-crime pictures they'd been emailed. The top one showed the naked torso of a young man, his head, what was left of it, lying in a dark pool of blood. The harsh lighting did nothing to lessen the brutal evidence of extreme violence against the person. The second picture was no easier to look at.

'I couldn't've shown a mother these, man . . .'

Standing back from the window, Sandra Tennant saw the police car finally drive off, aware that Mike was on the settee behind her, watching. She felt numb with shock, unable to make sense of the information she'd been given, of what those two men had come into her house and told her.

Paul – *little Pauly . . . her baby* – was dead?

It could not be.

She didn't want to turn round and have to deal with Mike, who was going to want her to reassure him that he'd had nothing to do with what had happened to Paul. Except that, if the man had only tried a *bit* bloody harder to get the boy to just tolerate him, he wouldn't't've stormed out and gone and got himself killed. Would he, Mike?

And then Sandra's mobile on the dresser started to ring. Some annoying tone Paul had downloaded and installed on to her phone and she'd never got round to asking him to change, because she didn't know how to do it herself.

'Want me to get that for you, Sandra?'

Sandra shook her head as she walked over to pick it up. It wasn't a number she recognised. She never took those calls and put the phone back down.

'I don't want to talk to anyone right now.'

They both stayed where they were, waiting for something – neither of them knew what and neither of them wanted to be the first one to talk about what they'd just been told. It was an event, a cataclysm, that showed up and magnified all the cracks in their relationship.

And then the house phone, the one in the hall, began to ring.

Sandra took a deep breath, turned round, glanced at Mike and started walking out of the room.

'Where you going?'

'To answer the phone, you never know . . .'

2

Tuesday 25th July, Gosforth, Newcastle Upon Tyne

Paul Hendry was standing, waiting for a bus, still jumpy and hyped from the massive, face-to-face shouting match he'd had with Mr Mike Bloody Tennant.

That was it.

The absolute and final straw.

Jee-*zus*! He'd had enough . . .

He was not going back to that house.

Ever.

Nervously twisting the silver ring on his little finger, Paul checked back in the direction he'd come, half expecting to see his mam's car driving his way, looking for him so she could persuade him to come home. He knew she'd forgive him. Even though he'd called Mike every name he could think of, and had then managed to break the window in the kitchen door when he'd slammed it on his way out.

Now *that* was what you called an exit, man!

That was goodbye in anyone's language.

He put his backpack on the pavement and leaned against the bus stop, letting what he'd said and done properly sink in. He really did not want to go back home – to the house he'd grown up in, *his* house, not that bloke's – as his mam was sure to try and make him apologise. And that was just not going to happen. But if he wasn't going to go back, where was he going?

Dave's would be no good as he'd been getting the distinct impression his mam was getting fed up of him and how much time he'd been spending there. Turning up at Dave's with a stuffed backpack wasn't going to work. And neither was going to his dad's right now, not since he'd got the new girlfriend. Cheryl. Blonde, young, only twenty-three, or something. Wait till his mam found out! Anyway, bunking over there in his dad's one-bedroom flat wasn't going to be on the cards until the gloss had worn off the old man a bit. Which left what?

In the distance he could see the bus approaching. The one that went past the Metro station, from where he could get right into town. It was too late in the day to put into action the plan he and Dave had been talking about, on and off, it seemed like for ever. The one about hitching down to London, the two of them. Except he kind of knew Dave was never really going to be up for it, not really. He was, though. *Now* he was.

The bus slowed to a halt, pulling up next to the stop. The doors hissed open and the driver looked down at him and then away again. A couple of old dears took their time getting off the bus, giving Paul a few more seconds of make-your-mind-up time. What the hell. He picked up his backpack and stepped up into the bus, paid the driver, took his ticket and made for a vacant double seat down the back. He'd rough it for the night. Just the night, mind. And tomorrow, in the morning, he'd get himself on to the London road, the A1(M) – he and Dave had spent hours looking at maps and stuff and he knew the route by heart now – and he'd get a lift. All the way to the Smoke.

Simple.

He'd spend the summer down south, get a job doing anything, find somewhere to kip. Maybe come back for the start of the autumn term, maybe not, he'd see how he got on. Why not? Ever since his parents had split, and then divorced, and what with his mam remarrying, it had been all about his parents doing things for themselves, to suit themselves, and nothing to do with him. Although they always said, whatever it was they were planning on doing, that it was for the best. Always for the best.

Paul stared out of the window, looking into the middle distance, somewhere between the glass, inches from his face, and the horizon. Thinking. Thinking that 'the best' was when his parents had been together and they were a proper family, and who cared if there were a few arguments? Everyone argued. Not everyone got divorced and then married some jerk called Mike Tennant. Or lived with a girl not *that* much older than their son. So now was the time for him to do something for himself. Make a clean break, have a fresh start of his own. For a bit, anyway. He could always come back, when and if he wanted to. On his own terms.

The bus pulled up at a stop and Paul, lost in thought, refocused on where he was. The Metro already! He grabbed his backpack from the seat next to him, made a dash for the exit doors, swung round the pole and jumped through the opening down on to the pavement. First step of the journey . . .

It was late now. He could tell without even looking at his watch, just something about the way the streets were. Empty. Echoey. Paul, wrapped in his sleeping bag and using his backpack for a pillow, turned to look over the flattened cardboard box he'd used to lie on and cover himself. Out on the street, from the narrow but quite deep entrance-way he'd chosen to bed down in, he couldn't see what or who had made the noise that must've woken him. He was about to roll back and try to get some more kip before he had to get up when he heard voices and what sounded like glass breaking.

Curiosity got the better of him, even though he knew he should probably mind his own business, and he quietly pushed the cardboard flat and shuffled as silently as he could to the edge of the shadows, towards the steps that led down to the pavement. He stopped when he saw the first figure. Standing, back to him, wearing black jeans and a dark hoodie with the hood up. Male? Female? He couldn't tell.

This person was a little way away, hands in pockets and weight on one leg, looking upwards. Paul followed where they were looking and saw a second hooded person, looked like a guy, making their way down a seven-metre-high post, on top of which were the smashed remains of a CCTV camera. He was using what looked like a wide leather belt to 'walk' down the post in small jumps, making it look so easy anyone could do it. As he reached the ground and unbuckled the belt, the second person took something out of the bag that was slung over their shoulder. Paul watched as they went over to the post and slapped a sticker on it, then dropped what looked like some pieces of orange paper on to the ground.

'Finished?' Paul heard the bloke whisper as he saw him stow the belt in a small black backpack, then pull a hammer out of his belt and stuff it in as well.

'Yeah . . .' The figure turned sideways, pushing their hood back. Paul could now see it was a girl, her profile white and stark in the street light. 'Neat work, Robbie!'

Paul rolled himself back into the shadows as they ran past, turning away just in case they spotted him. As their footsteps faded into the distance, he sat up in the dark, looking out into the silent, empty street and wondering who the hell the two of them were and what they were up to. They certainly weren't a couple of lagered-up scallies out for a laugh. They'd come prepared, and everything they'd done looked like it was practised, like they'd done it a few times before.

Paul unzipped his sleeping bag and got up, stretching the kinks out of his back. He walked over to the entrance and looked out left and then right. No one. He went down the steps and over to the post, bending down to pick up one of the pieces of orange paper; as he stood up he noticed the sticker, a white one, about ten by thirteen centimetres in size, stuck on lengthways and with two black letters printed on it. The first was a symbol, Ω, which he recognised as the Greek letter *omega*, and the other a capital P.

ΩP

What was *that* all about? Paul looked at the piece of paper he'd picked up. It was a small folded leaflet. He turned it round so he could read what it said. 'MANIFESTO 3' was printed across the top, in the kind of stencil typeface that made you think of armies and soldiers. Paul shrugged to himself and walked back up the steps to the entrance-way, wondering about what he'd seen, about the girl whose face he'd glimpsed. Fit-looking, with that flat sort of *EastEnders* accent. So different from the way the bloke she was with talked. He sat back down and held the pamphlet to the streetlight so he could read it.

Wherever you look there are cameras looking back AT YOU! There are 4 million of them. TRUE FACT. More EVERY DAY, spreading out from every town centre, blossoming like weeds on every road, pushing out through the tarmac arterial system across THE WHOLE COUNTRY. Word has it that they're actually using RPAs – remotely piloted aircraft, tiny pilotless drones – SPYPLANES equipped with all the latest tech, to increase coverage. It's a rumour, but with this lot in power, believe this: ABSOLUTELY ANYTHING'S POSSIBLE!

Supposed to make us all feel SAFER, they say. Supposed to CUT CRIME and CUT ROAD ACCIDENTS, they also say. Except we know it's really all about MONEY. And CONTROL, of course. You voted for them, you gave them the money and the control, and look what they did with it – put cameras EVERYWHERE, which are supposed to solve crime, but actually only move it elsewhere.

Paul stopped reading and turned to look at the front of the pamphlet again. Whoever had written it – the two he'd just seen trash the camera? – certainly seemed to think that getting out there and doing what they believed in was better than just talking about it. He started to read again.

Thing is, for too long most PEOPLE DIDN'T LOOK. They had no idea, until it was WAY TOO LATE. Now there's ONE CAMERA for every 14 people in the UK! And YOU are being WATCHED 24/7, almost wherever you go and whatever you are doing. There are a lot of things people NEVER NOTICE until it's too late.

Why aren't people doing anything? Why aren't you complaining, protesting, objecting, SHOWING YOUR DISAPPROVAL? If you don't like something, why just sit there and let it happen? **What has happened to the politics of the street?**

Paul reread the last two paragraphs, wondering what was meant by 'the politics of the street'. Did that mean rioting, or what? He understood the stuff about the cameras and being watched all the time, though. You saw them all over the place in the town, and his dad was always complaining about how many of them there were on the roads, put there, he said, to make money for fat-cat councillors and bugger all to do with road safety. He turned to the last page.

WE DON'T LIKE IT. And we are the ones who have decided to do something.

We are **OMEGA PLACE.**

We do not want to live as part of a monitored population. We do not want our faces on the world's biggest database. We want it to **STOP,** *and everything has to* **START** *somewhere.*

Because there's absolutely no telling where it'll all **END.**

3

Wednesday 26th July,
Graingertown, Newcastle Upon Tyne

ΩP. Omega Place. Neat logo, cool name, but what did it mean? As Paul wandered around, looking for a caff that was open at just after seven in the morning so he could get some breakfast, he thought about the kind of people who would set up an organisation dedicated to stamping out CCTV cameras.

Was it more of a useful thing to do than trying to stop fox hunting or setting test-lab rats and rabbits free? He didn't know what his opinion about that was. Were the cameras really such a big problem and were they worth getting nicked for? He didn't know, hadn't really ever given actual radical action much thought. He looked around him as he walked, wondering if what the writer had said was true, because there really did seem to be more cameras around now.

Like the leaflet said, wherever you looked, they were looking back at you.

Ever since he'd vacated his temporary sleeping quarters he couldn't help noticing them. All those little wired-up boxes staring at the world through their one solitary, black eye. Some of them even moved, like creepy robots, if you waited and watched long enough. He'd also noticed a couple more smashed cameras and quite a few ΩP stickers as he was walking. Those two had been busy. Or maybe there was a whole team of them. When he got to London he'd look out for stickers down there, see if they were working in more than one city.

London. Right. Better get on with the plan, once he'd got his mouth round a full English breakfast (not a waste of limited funds, he reasoned, as he'd no idea when he'd eat next). Straight after eating he was going to get himself out to where he could start hitching for a lift south. Paul's stomach growled at him, a reminder to get on with finding a caff, and he wondered how easy it would be getting a lift. He didn't look too untidy, considering, and all he could do was hope some lorry driver took a chance on him. And not some serial-killer maniac. That would be just his luck.

Turning into High Bridge he saw a small café with steamed-up windows and made straight for it, mouth watering at the thought of what he was about to order.

Having flicked through an abandoned copy of the *Sun* and read all the sport there was to read, Paul fished out the by now crumpled copy of Manifesto 3 and looked at it again. In his mind's eye he saw the cameras popping up, like the symptoms of a disease, all over the country, and wondered if it really was a fact that 'they' – Big Brother, the government, whoever – were using radio-piloted spyplanes with cameras on board. Sounded like something out of a crap Hollywood straight-to-vid movie, but you couldn't know for sure. Never say never, like his dad said.

After paying for his major breakfast, plus toast and two teas, and feeling well set up, he made his way over towards the Central Station. There'd be some public toilets where he could smarten himself up before he started hitching. For a fleeting moment he thought about home, where there'd be a shower, hot water, clean towels . . . and Mike Bloody Tennant.

Pushing the thought away he ignored the little red man on the crossing lights and made a dash for the other side of the street, earning himself an angry blast from the BMW that had to brake so it didn't hit him. Feeling somehow kind of bullet-proof, he crossed another road and went through the taxi rank into the station in search of the bogs.

It was about half nine when he eventually got to where he reckoned he could start hitching. Coming out of the station he looked around for which way to go for the road south. And there she was. He was sure of it. The girl from last night!

She was standing with her back to him, head turned so she was in profile. Like last night. Only her hood was down now, thick blonde hair pulled back in a loose ponytail, and in the daytime her features were softer than they'd seemed in the harsh street lighting. Definitely a looker. She was across the road and he'd just caught a glimpse as she'd gone into a shop, but he was sure it was her. Paul scanned the street but she didn't seem to be with her accomplice from the night before.

He didn't know exactly why he crossed the road and walked towards the shop, but he found himself on the other pavement and walking past the window, glancing to his right as he went by. He could see her, at the counter buying something. If it wasn't the same girl then it had to be her absolute double, right down to the same jeans, hoodie and bag. Carrying on along the pavement Paul stopped a few shops down and pretended to look in the window as he waited to see where the girl went when she came out.

Right. She turned right and was coming his way! He looked straight ahead and found himself looking at the woman behind the counter of the shop he was standing in front of. She was staring back at him with a half-puzzled, half-annoyed expression on her face, but he daren't look away just yet, not with the girl coming his way. And then she went past him. He smiled sheepishly at the woman in the shop and glanced to his left, waiting until the girl had walked far enough ahead for it not to appear too obvious that he was following her. Because that was exactly what he was going to do.

He was making this up as he went along, he knew it, but the irrational part of his brain made it sound like a great idea to find out more about this Omega Place thing. And all he had to do was follow this girl for a bit, then, when the time seemed right, then he'd make contact. Ask a few questions, get some answers and get on with the rest of his life. Go to the motorway, stick out his thumb and put some miles between him and Newcastle.

The girl turned right at the next corner and Paul slowed as he approached it, turning to follow her and just catching her as she disappeared into another shop. Walking up to it he saw it was a small newsagent's and she was at the counter at the back, looking at the display of sweets. Maybe, said the rational part of his brain, *maybe* you should just turn round and go off to start hitching and stop being so bloody stupid.

On the other hand, he could just check whether this was the same girl. You know, see if he could catch her saying something? Then he'd know. If he didn't, he'd always wonder whether it was her or not. Like that *really* mattered.

He found himself stepping inside the shop. Then he was slowly working his way down the display of magazines, desperately searching for something he could convincingly be found looking at – should the owner be checking him out, as he'd just noticed the small CCTV camera up in the far corner of the shop. But there just seemed to be women's magazines or top-shelf porno. He felt his armpits prickle as he broke out into a sweat. What the hell was he doing, making himself into a paranoid wreck when he should be away trying to get a lift?

'I'll have these and a T-Mobile top-up card, thanks.'

Paul stopped. That voice, the *EastEnders* accent. It *was* her. So, what did he do now? Talk to her here in the shop, or wait until she left and catch her up in the street? He quickly bent to pick up a newspaper from the ground-level display as she turned to go, and stood to find himself with a copy of *The People's Friend* in his hand. Dropping it like it was hot to the touch, Paul couldn't believe he was making such an exhibition of himself. If the girl hadn't noticed him before, she was bound to now.

'Can I help you, young man? Not a library here, you know.'

Paul glanced at the man behind the counter. 'Got any chewing gum?'

'Not down there with the papers, mate.'

'Yeah, right.' Paul walked down towards the counter, passing within a few centimetres of the girl, but studiously avoiding any eye contact, as she made her way out of the shop. He could hear her mobile start to ring as she stepped out on to the pavement and he grabbed a pack of gum from the display right in front of him, handing over a pound coin and accepting change in return. Stuffing the coins into his jeans pocket without bothering to check them, he opened the pack, folded a stick of gum into his mouth and left.

The overly sweet taste and slightly sickly aroma of some kind of fruit flavour filled his head. Which was what you got if you didn't pay attention. Back outside he saw the girl was some way down the street and, as nonchalantly as possible, he turned to go in the same direction. A minute or so later he heard her mobile go again and saw her take the call. Nice to be so popular, he thought. His phone hadn't rung once since the call from his mam last night, which he'd let go to voicemail rather than get involved in any kind of conversation that might persuade him out of what he fully intended doing. London or bust.

Up ahead Paul saw the girl stop at a junction to let a car pass before she crossed the road. Behind him he heard the whine of a gearbox being downshifted and a dusty, beat-up white Transit passed him, slowed some more and turned right, obscuring the girl from view. Instead of carrying on, as he expected it to, the van pulled up on the corner, the driver jumping out, running to the back and opening the rear doors, completely blocking his view of the pavement ahead.

Must be making a urgent delivery, Paul mused, reaching the junction himself and stopping to check before crossing. A random thought jack-in-the-boxed into his head. *He'd* got a licence. Driving lessons had been one of the things Mike Bloody Tennant had tried to use to get on his good side. He'd refused them at first, not wanting to let the man think he'd won any Brownie points or anything. But in the end he'd agreed to take them because his dad had said he'd be barmy not to – gift horse, and all that. Passed first time, too. Maybe he could get a job down in London, driving a van. Why not?

He was about to step off the pavement when a car com-ing down the road towards him swung into the side street, turning without indicating, the driver steering with one hand as he talked on his mobile. Paul looked at the car as it went away down the road, wondering what was the point of a law banning using mobiles in cars if no one gave a shit and just ignored it. He'd never heard of anyone getting done by the cops for it. Stupid, really.

As he walked round the Transit's open rear door he looked ahead to see how far away the girl was now and realised she was nowhere in sight. He frowned. Where could she have gone? Into a house? Well, if that was the case then he'd just wasted half an hour or more and he still had to get himself over to the motorway. He was aware of the fact that there was someone to his right – the driver of the Transit, who seemed to be taking ages to get whatever he was delivering out of the van – and then everything went black, like all his fuses had blown at once.

4

Wednesday 26th July, somewhere . . .

It was dark when Paul finally managed to open his eyes. He was lying on his front, on an old piece of carpet that smelled of oil, like a garage. His head hurt, he ached all over and something was taped across his mouth. And, when he tried to roll on to his back to see where he was, he found his wrists and ankles had been taped together as well.

Not part of the plan.

As his eyes adjusted to the lack of light, he realised he was in the back of a van. No . . . not *a* van, in the back of what had to be the crappy old white Transit that had pulled up opposite him as he was just about to cross over the road to follow that girl. The girl he'd seen last night. God, he knew that had been a stupid, crap, geeky, *stupid* bloody idea. So why had he done it? And why had someone cracked him over the head – what was *that* all about?

As he tried to manoeuvre himself into a more upright position, Paul realised that, while it was dark in the van, it was a bright, sunny day outside. He could see thin strips of white where the rear doors didn't fit properly.

Just as he'd managed to prop himself up against the side of the van he heard the sound of a door opening. Followed by a second one, with the van rocking, springs squeaking as people got in and slammed both of the front-cab doors shut almost simultaneously. So, there were two of them. At least. Paul breathed shallowly, waiting to see what happened next. Were they, whoever 'they' were, going to drive off with him? Or wait until it was night and *then* dump him?

Nothing happened next.

What were they doing? They were just the other side of a thin piece of sheet metal. He was sure he'd hear them if they were talking. Why were they just sitting there, and who was the second person anyway? Had there been two people in the van when it'd come towards him and turned into the side street? He hadn't paid that much attention to passing traffic as he wasn't expecting some delivery bloke to sock him on the back of his head and dump him in the back of his shitty van. That didn't happen, even in the rough parts of town.

'I still think it was bloody stupid . . .' A girl's voice, slightly muffled. *The* girl's voice? It was that flat London accent.

'He was following, man! Had to be done.' A bloke, sounded like the one voice from last night.

Paul frowned . . . it didn't compute . . . why would those two do this to him?

'Know what, Rob?' the girl said, a sarcastic edge to her voice. 'It didn't. Nothing *had* to be done by anyone.'

'Don't agree, man. Do *not* agree.'

'You're getting as paranoid as Sky and Orlando, know that?'

'Who was paranoid the other day? You were so sure we had some plainclothes bloke on our tail and it turned out he needed glasses and fancied you!'

'Look, you should've just left this one. What was he gonna do? Just some kid, ferchrissake . . .'

'We don't *know* that, Terri.'

In the back of the van Paul's jaw would've dropped, If his mouth hadn't been taped up. A kid! Bloody cheek!

'No, but we don't know he *isn't*, do we, Rob?'

'So let's ask him, shall we? See what the little creep's got to say for himself?'

One of the front-cab doors clunked open and someone got out.

Paul instinctively pushed himself away from the rear door, feeling mildly panicked – like what was this Rob guy going to do to him now? All he could do was wait, with his heart thudding and his breath starting to come in short, sharp bursts through his nose. And then the sliding side door of the van was pulled open. The one he was leaning against and hadn't realised was there. He fell backwards into blinding sunshine.

'*Shit!*'

Paul, aware that he was heading for the ground, felt hands grab him and push him back into the van. As he was unceremoniously dumped forward on to the van's floor he heard the sliding door being pulled back shut and the load space was plunged into darkness again.

There was a moment or two's silence as Paul lay, waiting, on the filthy carpet, aware that there was someone – Rob, presumably – standing over him, swearing under his breath. The other cab door opened and closed; gravel crunched as someone walked to the rear of the van. Paul saw one of the doors open part way and the girl appeared in the gap; pulling herself in, she turned to close the door.

'That was clever, Rob.'

'I didn't know he was there, did I? Wasn't where I put the little *shit*!'

Paul grunted as Rob took his frustration out with a kick.

'Leave it out, will you, Rob?'

'Did anyone see?'

'Don't think so . . .'

Paul felt the tape on his wrists being cut, hands, gentler ones this time, rolling him on to his back. He stared up at the shadowy figure of the girl he now knew was called Terri; glancing sideways he saw Rob, crouching, with his back to him, to his right. And Rob looked like he was rifling through his gear. Paul looked back at Terri as she leaned forward, reaching out with her right hand.

'This is going to sting like shit . . .' she said, as she ripped the tape off his mouth, almost pulling him up from the floor.

And she was right.

As he sat up, eyes shut, one hand clamped over skin that was red hot, it felt like his lips had been pulled off, along with whatever stubble the glue had stuck to.

'So, who the hell are you?'

Paul blinked and looked at Terri, squatting on her haunches in front of him.

'Were you following me?'

Paul took a deep breath and shrugged. What would be the point of lying now? Somehow they'd sussed what he was doing. They knew.

'Yeah,' he nodded. 'I was.'

'Why?'

Another shrug.

'I just looked in his backpack, Terri . . . he's got a Manifesto. He knows who we are. So who's paranoid now, sis?'

Terri sat down, cross-legged, and started rolling a cigarette. 'What's your name?'

'Paul . . . Paul Hendry.'

'Well, Paul Hendry, what gives? I mean, what *are* you up to?'

'Nothing. I just saw you last night, in Grainger, doing that camera.'

'And you followed us out here? How'd you manage to do that?'

'I didn't . . . it was an accident, right?'

Rob punched Paul's arm, hard. 'Accident? How can you follow someone by *accident*, man?'

'Yeah, Paul.' Terri flicked a disposable lighter and lit her roll-up. 'Explain that one.'

Paul looked from Terri to Rob, then glanced around the back of the Transit. Outside, in the world beyond this white metal box, life was carrying on like normal. If he hadn't been so stupid he'd probably be on his way to London by now, not stuck here with gaffer tape wrapped round his ankles and feeling like a total prat. Explain what he'd done? How could he? He'd no idea himself. He sighed and shook his head.

'Like I said, I saw you guys last night. I was in some door-way, sleeping rough, and you woke me up, OK? When you'd gone I went and got one of the leaflets.' Paul leaned forward. 'Can you cut the stuff round my feet, too?'

Terri shook her head. 'Later . . . carry on, Paul Hendry.'

Paul frowned.

'The rest of the story, man.' Rob pushed him.

Paul shouldered his hand off. 'OK! Gimme a chance, right?' This Rob guy was getting on his nerves. So he waited for a moment before carrying on. 'I was on my way to hitch a lift to London when I saw you.' He nodded at Terri.

She blew smoke at him. 'And?'

'And . . . you know, I'd read that Manifesto thing.' He did *not* want to say something as lame as he'd followed her because he thought she looked fit. Then, it seemed like even before he'd thought them, the words just sort of fell out of his mouth. 'And I was, you know, kind of wondering how you joined.'

'Joined?'

'Omega Place?'

Paul couldn't believe he'd said it, and Terri and Rob didn't look exactly convinced either. What was he on? Maybe that's what happened when someone cracked your skull.

Rob snorted. 'You read one pamphlet you pick up in the street and you want to drop everything and go to the front line? Where are you coming from, man?'

'Didn't take Sky long to convince you to come along for the ride, Rob, the way he tells it.'

'I was out there already, me.'

Terri ignored the comment and waved her plastic pouch of tobacco at Paul. 'Smoke?' He shook his head. 'Been on the street long?'

'Not long.' Which was true.

'And you're on your way to London . . . how old are you?'

'Eighteen.' Well, nearly.

'Anyone after you, cops and stuff?'

'No.' Hopefully not. But there was no knowing what his mam had done.

'And you fancy getting into some radical action.' It was a statement, not a question, and Terri wasn't looking at him as she spoke. 'Rob?' she said, nodding towards the rear door as she got up.

'Want me to put some tape back on his trap?'

Terri stopped as she opened the door. She glanced at

34

Paul. 'Make a sound and you'll get a kicking.'

Rob smirked at him as he got out, pushing the door to and leaving him on his own again. What were they up to now? Deciding his future? One of the reasons he'd never got on with Mike Bloody Tennant was that he was always trying to give him advice and tell him what to do. If he'd wanted advice he'd have asked for it . . .

Paul started picking at the frayed end of the silver-grey tape wrapped God knew how many times round his ankles. Would he get a kicking if he took the stuff off? Once he'd got rid of it he'd give Rob a good kicking if he tried anything else on. He would. Cursing himself for still biting his nails, he worked small bits of the gaffer tape up until he had enough to get a hold of and then he started pulling.

As the tape unravelled he wondered where he was. Concentrating on listening as hard as he could to see if he was able to work anything out, he ripped the tape back. There was a bit of traffic noise, not much, and not very near, and just something about the sounds from outside that he'd picked up the couple of times the van door had opened that made him think they were somewhere exposed. The top of a multi-storey car park, maybe. Somewhere nice and high they could throw him off.

Which was when the handle on the van door turned and Paul, with a couple of feet more tape to undo, looked up to see Terri, one eyebrow raised, looking back at him.

'Pins and needles?' he said, hoping he sounded convincing. 'My feet've gone to sleep.'

Terri got in. No sign of Rob. 'Wait a sec . . .' She got out a clasp knife and cut through the remaining tape.

'Thanks.' Paul pulled the tape off his jeans and waggled his feet. 'Better.'

'I'm sure.'

Paul allowed himself to relax slightly. 'What . . . you know . . . what's going to happen?'

'Good question. What d'you *want* to happen?'

'Me?'

Terri nodded.

'Until this morning, I just wanted to get to London. Get a job driving a van or something and –'

'You got a licence?' Terri took her Golden Virginia out again. 'Full?'

'Yeah.'

She nodded to herself. 'So you go to London, get a job, and . . . ?'

'And I dunno. Then I read that leaflet and I thought maybe what you're doing would be good.'

'Maybe or really?'

'Why?'

'Why what?'

'Why all the questions?'

'Because . . .' Terri finished making the cigarette and lit it. 'Because I think we need an extra face, and you might be it. You could fit.'

The realisation that he had absolutely no idea what he was letting himself in for blossomed in Paul's head. He didn't know these people from a hole in the ground and here he was seriously thinking about going off with them.

'What does Rob say?'

'Rob? Rob thinks you're a waste of space, but he thinks everyone but him's crap. I don't believe our Rob has ever had a moment's self-doubt in his entire life.'

'Where is he now?'

'Finding somewhere to take a piss.'

'Where are we?'

'Now? Up by that big statue, the one with the wings.'

'The Angel of the North?'

'Yeah, there.'

'So why d'you need an extra face, and why d'you think I could be it, then?'

'You look like you can handle yourself. And you're disposable, like the rest of us.'

'I am?'

'True. You're out here on your own, no ties, invisible. Just the kind Orlando looks for . . . I'm sure he'll like you.'

'Who's Orlando?'

There was a loud click and the side door of the van slid back to reveal a grinning Rob. Behind him, on top of a gentle, green rise, Paul saw the Angel, huge ribbed wings outstretched and facing south. The way he wanted to go.

'Orlando's the boss, man.' Rob climbed in and pulled the door shut behind him. 'And he's gonna spit bricks if we turn up with you in tow.'

'We'll try him out in Leeds, on the way back.' Terri looked at Paul as she stubbed her cigarette out on the metal floor. 'If he's no good, we'll leave him there.'

5

Wednesday 26th July, Southgate, north London

The hush of very early morning noises – distant bird calls, the whine of a milk float's electric motor, the occasional passing car – was jarred by the sharp, brittle sound of the pane of glass in a suburban front door being shattered by a hammer. Nearby a dog started barking in response.

'Was that completely necessary, Drake?'

Tony Drake looked down at the short, overweight man standing next to him. His arsey client, Derek Taylor, the owner of the property. He'd hired Drake Security Services, in their capacity as bailiffs, to get the house back off the poxy squatters who'd taken it over a few months before.

'They've had a notice of eviction, knew we was coming, and they've gone, Mr Taylor. And they've changed all the locks . . . so we had to break something to get in, didn't we?' Tony looked over at the two uniforms who'd turned up the same time they had. 'Why'd you get the law involved?'

'Better safe than sorry. You never know, do you?'

Tony knew all right. Derek Taylor was a Mason and one of his pals at the local Lodge must have done him a favour. Look after their own, that lot. He glanced at the house, a not-so-neat-any-more end of terrace he also knew was part of Taylor's extensive, if low-rent, property portfolio. Squatters were what went with the territory if you let anywhere like this stay empty for too long.

'Are you coming in, Mr Taylor?' Tony gestured towards the house, its door now pushed open; his two men had gone inside and he ought to be there himself to check everything was A-OK and to see the locks were changed again, the glass replaced and the place was properly shut up tight before they left.

'No.' Taylor shook his head, turning to the two policemen. 'Sergeant?'

One of them looked his way and then they both walked over.

'We're constables, actually, sir.'

'Would you mind just giving the place the once-over? I'm sure Mr Drake will be grateful for the extra eyes.'

Tony walked off, the two plods in tow on their make-work task, thanking whoever it was up there in the cosmos looking out for him that he didn't have a stupid twat like Derek Taylor as a landlord.

6

Friday 28th July, Thames House, London

Deputy Section Manager Jane Mercer picked up the note attached to the folder she'd just been sent by the Director of Internal Affairs at MI5, Alex Markham, no less, and read it again. 'Your thoughts. ASAP.' She opened the folder and looked at its contents – a handful of black and white stickers with the characters ΩP printed on them in one plastic bag and a couple of orange A5 leaflets that declared themselves to be something called 'Manifesto 3' in another, plus a report from Steven Pearce in Threat Evaluation. Her thoughts, as soon as possible. So she'd better get started. Reaching for the report, she began reading.

The stickers and the pamphlets had been found in a squat up in Southgate on the morning of the twenty-sixth, two days ago. A couple of uniforms had gone in with the bailiffs, although no reasons given as to why that had been deemed necessary, and the contents of the folder had been found behind a chest of drawers in an upstairs room that appeared to have been used as a print shop. The computers and laserjets had gone, but the discarded cartridges and spilled toner dust had been a dead giveaway.

The whole of the house had been cleaned out, and appeared, so the report said, to have been wiped down. Which was odd for a squat.

One of the uniforms, obviously destined for greater things, had given the place an extra going-over, just because it was so strange to see a squat that had actually been cleaned up. If they were trying so hard to hide something, maybe they'd been careless and left something behind. It was good thinking and had turned up the stuff in the plastic bags.

As soon as the contents of the leaflet had been read, the whole thing had been wrapped up and sent to MI5, and then to Threat Evaluation, which did exactly what it said on the box . . . evaluate threats, grade them and then tell the people who actually dealt with the face-to-face stuff whether they had anything to worry about. And at first glance, on a scale of one to ten, Mercer did not think there was too much sleep to be lost over Omega Place. It all looked a bit amateur hour and she'd yet to see quite why Markham had got involved. But she'd be thorough, like the constable, and see what she could tease out of the material that had been sent down to her.

She picked up her phone and dialled an internal extension, frowning as voicemail kicked in. Replacing the handset she fished her mobile out of her bag and speed-dialled a number.

'Ray, will you stop chatting up the blonde from the fourth floor . . . OK, the brunette, whoever. Fag break over, Mr Salter. I need your expertise and I need it now.'

Mercer snapped her phone shut and, while she waited for her assistant, fiddled with the mouse on her desk until the screen of her computer cleared. Just because she hadn't heard of Omega Place didn't mean they hadn't already been caught and logged by another part of the MI5 web.

She keyed in her password and had searched through a

couple of databases, with no results, by the time Salter, and a haze of peppermint-flavoured tobacco smoke, came into the room.

'Do you only go out with women who smoke, or are your charms enough to make them forget you smell like a mentholated ashtray?'

'I've told you before, I only smoke so that at least one of us is up to speed with office gossip, boss.' Salter pulled out a chair and sat down. 'Otherwise we'd have to rely on internal emails, and we both know there's nothing interesting in them as they're all scanned by the über-spooks. So, what's up, Doc?'

'While I ferret around on the web, I want you to take these over to the forensic guys and see if there are any prints, any anything, in fact, on them.' Mercer pushed the folder containing the plastic bags across her desk.

Mercer sat back and picked up the copy of Manifesto 3 she'd kept. After reading it through a couple of times she put it back down on her desk and stared out of her window. It was hard to argue with the fact that there was a lot of CCTV, but it was there for a reason and she could definitely argue with the author's reasons – twisted logic, more like – for opposing it.

There was only one thing that really niggled. How the hell did these people know about the RPAs? The remotely piloted, camera-carrying drones were experimental. To all intents and purposes, they and the test programme that was underway didn't exist. For that reason alone, this lot were worth a good look.

But, whatever Omega Place was, it didn't have much of a presence, which in Mercer's experience either meant it was small and insignificant, or that it was a big organisation that was trying to *look* small and insignificant. The minimal amount of info she'd been able to glean pointed towards the former, with it possibly being some extreme civil liberties outfit. What an old boss had once described as the three 'U's – under-funded, ultra-left and up their own arses. She had found some evidence on the Net that they'd been active in various parts of the country, which might, of course, mean a number of cells were operating, but, then again, might not.

Sometimes her job drove her mad.

She wasn't a big fan of blue-sky thinking, coming up with ideas based on little more than conjecture and gut feeling. She liked facts. Hard facts, and the more of them the better.

She was on a fishing expedition, out in the unpoliced badlands of the Net, where anyone could post anything and there was no absolute way of differentiating lies from the truth, when Ray Salter knocked on her office door and came in without waiting for an answer. He was smiling.

'You have news, and by the smirk on your face I'd say you're classifying it as Good News.'

Salter nodded as he sat down. 'There were some prints, in fact a couple of fairly clean ones.'

'And?'

'And one of them has a name attached to it.'

'Which is?'

'James Baker.'

Mercer rubbed her eyes, gritty from staring for too long at a screen. 'So . . . James Baker. Apart from the fact that, at some time in his life, he did something that got him arrested, what else have you got to tell me? Who is he and why did he get picked up by plod?'

'Riot Squad, actually.'

'*Riot* Squad?'

'Yeah, he was nabbed during the poll-tax demos, back in 1990.'

Mercer sat up, frowning. 'Any more details?'

Salter took a couple of sheets of paper out of the folder he was carrying and scanned them. 'Not a lot. Born in 1968, in Slough . . . makes him, um . . .'

'Thirty-eight.'

'Right, thirty-eight . . . so, born in Slough, where he lived until '86 when he went to Birmingham to study politics. He was arrested somewhere off Trafalgar Square on March the thirty-first, 1990 . . . suspicion of looting, aggravated assault and various other charges under the Riot Act.' Salter held up a very grainy black and white photo of a chaotic street scene, baton-wielding police and demonstrators in what looked like an aggressive stand-off. 'James Baker's in there, somewhere, apparently. Anyway, he was kept on remand so long that by the time his case came up he'd been inside longer than if he'd been sentenced.'

'Is that it?'

Salter nodded. 'His only mention in the annals of crime and punishment. Maybe he learnt his lesson, been a good boy since then.'

'Until his dabs appear on this stuff from the squat. No other prints?'

'None that were of any use.'

'Wonder what he's been up to for the last sixteen years, our Mr Baker. Did the lab get anything else off that stuff?'

'Both the stickers and the orange paper can be bought in any high street stationer's, and the printing is standard laserjet output. No distinguishing features.' Salter tipped back his chair and rocked to and fro. 'You think this lot are worth worrying about, then, boss?'

'Upstairs are interested.'

'The RPAs?'

'Bull's eye. This Omega Place lot are definitely worth looking at. Political activism and state secrets are two things that definitely don't go well together . . .'

*　　*　　*

INTERNAL MEMO – FOR YOUR EYES ONLY

FROM:	Alex Markham, Dir. Int. Affairs, MI5
TO:	Michael Turner, PPS Home Secretary
DATE:	28/7/06
REF No.:	DF5002.40.70/1.1V
PRIORITY:	**HIGHEST**
Re:	Material found at a Southgate address, passed on to us by the Met.

Michael,

The attached material came to light during the repossession of a property by bailiffs, spotted by an eagle-eyed uniform. It came, fairly swiftly for these things, to Threat Evaluation, here at Thames House.

My only reason for involving you in this is the mention of the RPAs, about which I think there should be a meeting.

Please advise the Home Office response ASAP.

Yrs

Alex

From the desk of Michael Turner

Alex,

The Home Secretary is, understandably, extremely worried by the implications contained in this so-called Manifesto 3, as well as by the actions of these people (BTW, do we have examples of Manifestos 1 and 2? If so, could we please have copies). This kind of grassroots unrest is exactly the kind of thing we don't need at the moment.

The mention of the RPAs is particularly unsettling, and the HS would like to meet with you and discuss how these people can be shut down forthwith, if not sooner, to quote. There has been mention of setting up a taskforce.

My view is that we don't want to overreact to events. We all know what can happen when perceived threats are dealt with a little too enthusiastically. That being the case, I thought you might like a 'heads-up' re this taskforce idea, in advance of the meeting.

I look forward to your thoughts.

Michael

7

Thursday 27th July, the outskirts of Leeds

Paul sat in the middle, between Rob, who'd taken over the driving at the last stop, and Terri. They were in a new van, having dumped the white Transit at a service station car park the night before and replaced it with a nondescript blue van.

He had to admit that these two had their business down. Stealing the van had been done like a military operation, right down to changing the number plates. It was no more than five minutes from the time they'd parked up, after doing a quick circuit of the car park to check the place out and choose the van they wanted to take, to the moment they were back on the motorway.

Rob had told him to stay in the Transit and wait for his signal – a sharp whistle – before coming over, walking, not running, to the new van. All he'd had to do was keep an eye out for anyone walking or driving their way; if he spotted anyone, Terri had said, he should get out of the van, opening and closing the door twice. But no one had come.

And now here they were, approaching Leeds. The furthest south he'd ever been, in England anyway. He'd gone to Spain a few times on holiday, back in the day, before the divorce, but if they took him on to London it would be his first time there. Part of him, the scared, nervous part, couldn't believe what he'd done. Instead of taking the first opportunity to get away from these people he'd only *asked* to go *with* them!

But everything had happened so fast. And it was exciting, being with Terri and Rob, even if Rob was a bit of a dickhead. They were pretty out there, these two; like renegades, really, beyond the law. And why the hell not? At least they believed in something and weren't just sitting round letting stuff happen. He was doing something as well, not stuck back at home thinking about it. Like Dave. And here he was, driving around in a stolen vehicle, about to get even more involved. He must be cracked . . .

'You going to set me like a test or something?'

'Yeah.' Rob looked across at Terri, grinning. 'GCSE Post Climbing and Camera Smashing! Now if they'd had *them* at my school I might've passed an exam or two.'

'We're gonna have to see how fit you are,' Terri yawned. 'And whether you can cut it under pressure.'

Paul, like he'd caught it from Terri, yawned too; all three of them had had a fairly uncomfortable night, sleeping in the van in a lay-by.

'You never explained why you needed someone else.'

Terri's turn to glance over at Rob.

'You never told him, Terri?'

'Told him what?'

'About Jez, man.'

'No, I didn't. Yet.'

'Who's Jez?'

Terri started rolling a fag, something Paul had noticed she did when she wanted time to think. He waited for her to say something, to add another small jigsaw piece to the puzzle, because he still didn't know very much about

48

Omega Place. So far there were just the names. Terri Hyde, Rob Gillespie, and they'd mentioned someone called Orlando. Orlando Welles, he thought that was it, who they talked about like he was the boss. And someone called Sky, an older bloke, a Yank. And if he'd remembered right there was another girl – Izzy? – and a bloke, Tommy. But that was it, the sum total of what he knew about these people.

'Jez was diamond.' Terri pinched strands of tobacco from each end of the roll-up, carefully putting them back in the pouch and resealing it. 'The best.'

'Was?'

'Yeah, "was". He karked it, man.' Rob made a diving motion with his left hand. 'He's not the best now.'

'Shut it, Rob.'

Paul looked out of the windscreen, watching the streets and shops and cars go by. 'Suicide?'

'What? Course not. It was an accident.' Terri lit her cigarette. 'He was up on a roof, doing some cameras, and he got spotted. There was a chase, he made a mistake, slipped and fell. Ten, maybe fifteen metres. There was no way he could've survived that. And Sky watched it happen, there was nothing he could do . . . had to leave him there, on the pavement. Alone.'

'He was dead, sis. And if it happened to me, right? If it happened to me, God forbid,' Rob crossed himself, 'you'd have to leave me an all. That's the way it is. That's what Orlando's always said . . . even if you only break something, you get left.'

'Yeah, that's what he always says, but Orlando hardly ever goes out to do stuff, does he? He's not going to have to deal with it like we are, is he, Rob?'

'He's the brains, isn't he . . . makes the plans for us to do.'

49

'What am I going to have to do?'

'Shitting yourself, now, Pauly?' Rob checked his mirrors and indicated that he was pulling over into the left lane. 'Sure you want to join us? You can get out here, pick up another lift. No problem, mate.'

Paul said nothing, chewing his lip and watching as Rob drove into a McDonald's car park. Whatever it was they were going to ask him to have a go at, he swore to himself he was going to show the mouthy bastard behind the wheel that he could do it. He was fit enough, didn't smoke and trained pretty much twice a week with the football team. And he wasn't afraid of heights . . . didn't think he was, anyway.

The van pulled up with a squeal of brakes.

'Are we eating in or out, sis?'

'Out.' Terri rolled up her window and opened the door. 'I need to stretch my legs. Come on, Paul, we'll go and queue. You want your usual, Rob?'

'Yeah.'

Paul watched the van drive off. 'Why does he call you "sis"? He's not your brother, is he?'

'No!'

'Well, why then?'

'D'you like being called Pauly?'

'No, not really. It's what me mam calls me.'

'Same thing with me, my brother always called me sis. Somehow, God knows how, he works out exactly what you *don't* want to be called, calls you that *all* the bloody time, and then everyone else starts doing it too. It's like a really annoying talent.'

'How old is he?'

'He *says* he's twenty-one, but he lies about everything

else, so we know that's probably not true.' Terri went in through the double doors, holding one open for Paul. 'I reckon he's your age . . . Sky says he's sure he was around sixteen when he met him and that was a year or so ago.'

'Where'd they meet?'

'Glastonbury . . . Rob was nicking stuff. He's very good at it, but Sky's better at spotting someone doing it. What d'you want?'

Paul took the change out of his pocket to see what he had.

'I'm paying. We get expenses when we're on the road, so save your money.'

'You sure?'

'Straight up.'

Straight up. Paul was staring at the camera Terri and Paul had chosen for him to put out of action. It was right at the top of a six-metre-high pole – too far away, apparently, to use their high-powered, super-soaker water pistol, convert- ed to fire emulsion paint, and way too far from any easily accessible buildings to drop bricks from. He was going to have to climb. Not right to the top, just as far as the cable. The one he was going to have to cut through with a pair of heavy-duty, insulated clippers. Still and all, high enough.

Once the camera had been located Rob had driven around till he'd found what he was looking for: some out-of-the-way place where nobody would disturb them for an hour or so. Which was how Paul had got his first and only lesson in pole climbing before he had to do it for real.

And now, here he was. About to do it. For real.

Jee-zus.

'OK, Pauly . . .' Rob looked at his watch, then up and

down the empty street. 'Time to go.'

'You'll be fine,' Terri nodded, a half-smile on her lips. 'The first couple of metres'll be a doddle cos they've put that anti-sticker paint on. Great for grip.'

Standing in the shadows of a doorway on the opposite side of the street to the camera, Paul hefted the leather harness Rob had taught him how to use and felt his stomach knot as he broke out into a nervous sweat. He could do this. He could do this . . .

Leaving the safety of the deep shadows, Paul loped across the road, the cutters, swinging on a nylon lanyard, thumping on his chest like an extra heartbeat. It was three in the morning. He was about to climb up a post and cut the cable to a CCTV camera. He must need his bloody head examining, he really must. He stopped in front of the post and, like Rob had showed him, stepped into the harness, swung the belt part around the pole and did it up.

Too loose . . .

As the seconds ticked by, the blood singing in his ears, sweat running down his face, he undid the straps and pulled them tighter. Not too tight. He tested the belt.

Fine.

HERE WE GO!

He hitched the belt upwards, leaned back, using his own weight to create tension, then climbed up. Jerking himself forward, Paul swung the belt up again and climbed some more – step and repeat, step and repeat. And don't look down. He looked up instead and saw the cable that was his ultimate target snaking in a loop down from the camera, which was pointing at a crossroads to his left. He only had a couple of metres to go. Easy.

And then his foot slipped.

He hadn't been paying attention. Hadn't noticed that he was on smooth metal now, not the rougher surface he'd started climbing on. He fell, in that way you do when you're almost asleep, but not quite, and your whole body jerks. Only an inch or so, but the shock almost froze the sweat on him.

He tried to steady himself, and then he so nearly made the classic error Rob had warned him about – grabbing for the pole instead of pushing back. What had Rob drummed into him that he had to do? Keep the triangle? That was it, *he had to keep the triangle*!

The pole, the belt, him: the triangle.

It was geometry, only it wasn't on paper, it was hanging in the air. Paul pushed back and steadied himself. Took a deep breath and carried on upwards. The only way to go.

Then the cable was there, right in front of him. He could stop. Stop climbing, anyway. He was about to get the clippers and get the job done when he heard the whistle. Terri's warning sign. It meant that either there was a car or a person approaching and he was to do nothing, stay where he was. If he'd been nearer the ground he was supposed to get down as fast as possible and just stand by the post. This high up it was best, Rob had said, to do nothing. People rarely looked up, he'd said.

Well, he'd soon find out if that was true.

It was a car. He could hear it now. Terri must've spotted its headlights. Paul risked a glance down and saw it come round the corner quite slowly and for seconds he was sure whoever was in the car was going to look straight up at him. Instead the driver simply accelerated and drove on, and he realised he'd been holding his breath – like anyone could hear him from where he was. Wiping his hand on his jeans, Paul fumbled for the cutters' thick, rubberised grips. Do it quick, Rob had said, and don't touch the cable once it's cut. One of the wires was the power supply.

Reaching over, Paul positioned the curved blades, counted to three and did the deed. To his surprise the cutter sliced through the cable far more easily than he'd expected, the wires falling apart and one of them coming dangerously close to his face. Letting the cutter swing, he grinned to himself. He'd done it!

All he had to do now was get back down.

8

Friday 28th July, Thames House

Jane Mercer had a feeling in the pit of her stomach about this meeting. Under normal circumstances, if it was just a simple briefing, it would be done by someone other than the director. Ergo these weren't normal circumstances, neither was it just a simple briefing, but she couldn't see why. Whatever the reasons, this looked as if it could be a real opportunity for her – why else would a Deputy Section Manager have been given the file?

As she turned right out of the lift and went through the doors into the director's outer office she wondered why, if someone was going to leak classified information, they hadn't leaked it to an organisation people might listen to. You could probably count the number of readers of Manifesto 3 on the fingers of one hand.

Markham's PA looked up as Mercer came in and nodded slightly. 'He's waiting for you, Jane.'

'OK . . .' Mercer nodded back, giving the door a light knock, waiting for a second and then going in.

'Ah, Jane, thanks for coming.' Alex Markham, Director of Internal Affairs, indicated that she should sit down. 'I've just come back from a meeting with the Home Secretary.'

'Yes, sir?'

'Main topic of conversation . . .' Markham picked up a folder from his desk and set it down again. 'The report on this Omega Place. It's rung alarm bells, at least it has in the Home Office, with the Counter-Terrorism and Intelligence mob, at least.'

'It's the mention of the remotely piloted aircraft, isn't it?'

'Correct. Have you got anything else to tell me about who we may be dealing with?'

Mercer shook her head. 'We've come up with nothing, really. Just that name, James Baker, whom we're assuming's involved because we found his prints on one of the stickers.'

'Do we know any more about him?'

'No, just that he was arrested during the poll-tax riots back in 1990, but we can find no record of him since then. It's like he doesn't exist any more . . . no income tax, no National Insurance, nothing on the radar at all.'

'Odd . . .'

'We could do deep background on him, if you want.'

'You think there's a problem, that there's something there to find?'

Mercer shook her head. 'Not really, sir. He's probably a small-time activist of some sort.'

'A bloody well-connected activist. The RPA programme is anything *but* public knowledge and the powers that be would very much like it to stay that way.' Markham sat back in his leather chair and steepled his fingers. 'There were some seriously overactive imaginations at work this afternoon, I can tell you. One of them, some Counter-Terrorist suit . . . Henry Garden, I think it was . . . he was pointing the finger at everyone from radical Islamists to eastern European terror groups.'

'Really?'

'I do not exaggerate, believe me.'

56

'What d'you want me to do? The barrel's pretty much scraped and empty at this point. Threat evaluated.'

'Understood, Mercer, absolutely understood.' Markham leaned forward and flicked open a second folder on the desk in front of him. 'But they want us to set up a special taskforce to close these people down, whoever they are, for good. I've decided to put you in charge.'

'Me, sir?'

'Yes. Find them and shut them down – and the leak . . . find out where it's coming from, will you? I've made arrangements for you to have another office and extra staff.' Markham closed the folders and checked his watch. 'I want you to hit the ground running with this on Monday.'

'Thank you, sir.' Mercer got up. 'Will that be all, sir?'

'Yes.' Markham nodded, pushing the folders across his desk. 'Oh, there is one other thing.'

'Sir?'

'Any idea why it's called Omega Place? Odd sort of name for people like that. They normally use some tortuous acronym or other.'

'No idea, sir, but I'll have it looked into.'

'Why don't you do that.' Markham began tidying his desk. 'It would be interesting to know . . .'

Henry Garden paced his office. He hadn't smoked a cigarette in he couldn't remember how long. Years. Decades, even. He'd given up, broken that particular habit, chucked it. But the one thing he wanted right now was to light up. Instead, he was wearing out carpet and chewing a nail. Another thing he thought he'd given up doing.

What a *great* way to start back at work after a week's break. God, how he wished he was back in Las Vegas. If he'd taken two weeks off – ten days even – he wouldn't have to be dealing with this crap right now. It would be someone else's responsibility and nothing to do with him. Until later. The trouble was, in this world there was always a later . . . nothing ever went away for good.

Right there in the middle of the bloody meeting with that spook Markham was when it had happened . . . when the MI5 Director had taken out a folder and started briefing the Home Secretary on Omega Place. At the time, Garden had thought he was going to spit out the biscuit he was eating and had had to make out he was choking. Everyone else round the table was enquiring how Omega Place knew about the RPA programme, while what he was asking himself was how the bloody, *bloody* hell did *they* know about Omega Place?

Because, as far as he understood, it didn't really exist.

He'd tried putting up a couple of smokescreens, about them possibly being foreign nationals of some sort – Arab, one of the 'Stans or whatever – but no one paid much attention. Except Markham, who'd given him a strange look, like he'd just noticed he was there and was wondering who he might be. In Garden's experience the last thing you wanted was to be noticed by people like Markham, so he mostly kept his mouth shut for the rest of the meeting. All that he could think was that, whatever was going on, something appeared to have gone a bit pear-shaped.

More than a bit.

And as Nick delighted in reminding him, 'When there's shit to clear up, Henry Garden's the man whose job it is to pick up the shovel!'. Or, right now, the phone. Nick would really want to know about this. The question was, what was the best way of getting in touch with him? Certainly not an office landline, or email.

Garden looked at his watch, and then consulted his BlackBerry. This was a set of circumstances he'd hoped and prayed he'd never have to deal with – a potential collision between the office and his very private life – but he did have a ten-minute window. He would use it to take a quick walk.

Henry Garden had been a not-very civil servant all his life, climbing up the greasy pole using a successful mixture of administrative talent (medium) and an attentive, unctuous servility (major) to get to where he was today: a divisional manager at the Home Office. For a time at school his nick-name had been Grovel, which he'd hated and had worked extremely hard to eradicate, but, if put under extreme pressure, he would have to admit to its pinpoint accuracy. Children could be so damn cruel, one of many reasons he was so very glad he didn't have any.

As soon as he was out of sight of the office he speed-dialled Nick Harvey's mobile number. And got voicemail. Bloody typical. The man *never* answered the phone, like it would be committing some huge moral crime if he was ever available. Henry knew that for a person in his position in public service (especially a person with what some might call an overfondness for games of chance) to have anything to do with a man like Nick was asking for trouble, which was why he'd gone for a walk to make the call. There was absolutely no way of knowing what or who they were listening to at work, when work was the Counter-Terrorism and Intelligence Directorate. As his dear, departed mother always used to say: better be safe than sorry.

9

Saturday 29th July, M6 southbound

Paul glanced at the dashboard. They were getting pretty low on petrol, not low enough for the light to flash on the gauge, but time, in his opinion, to fill up. He'd been driving for the last couple of hours, Rob catnapping up front with him, Terri now spark out in the back of the van.

Rob had just handed over the keys at the last major stop and said it was his turn at the wheel. Another little test, obviously. See if the new kid really could drive. Paul had taken the keys with the silent mantra 'please, please, *please* don't let me stall!' repeating in his head like a stuck record. He'd had his licence for less than six months and the only car he'd ever properly driven was his mam's six-year-old Fiesta, all 1.1 litres of it.

Starting the van had been, if anything, even more nerve-wracking than getting up the pole and doing the camera. With Terri sitting right next to him, and Rob grinning his sly, tricky grin, he'd truly felt the pressure. He'd stalled, of course, but thank God not until about a mile or so after setting off, at a set of lights. Now that he'd got – he looked at the trip meter – almost 150 miles behind him, he felt much more relaxed. And he wasn't gripping the steering wheel like it was a lifebelt any more.

'Rob? You awake?'

A grunt. Silence. Then Rob yawned. 'Am now . . . wha'd'you want?'

'We'll need petrol soon. Shall I stop at the next service station?'

Rob slid across the seat and looked at the dash. 'Yeah, better had, man.'

Since his successful debut back in Leeds – one camera deactivated, one point made – Paul could feel that Rob had been treating him as less of a waste of space. Whether he was totally convinced Terri was doing the right thing in bringing him with them was hard to tell. It was like being in the playground at primary school trying to work out if you were going to be accepted into the cool gang, allowed to play football in the only team that mattered. He'd hated that feeling then and he didn't much care for it now.

He'd half thought that, if he passed the first test, he might, having proved his point, just say *adios* and bugger off. After all, he'd only really put himself through it, climbed that pole and cut the cable, to show Rob he was wrong. And prove Terri had been right, of course . . . that had been important.

But as soon as he'd done it, and got back down to the pavement, he'd experienced such a rush he felt like going and finding another camera to do – right there and then! They hadn't let him, which was probably just as well as he would no doubt have screwed it up with a massive dose of over-confidence. The thing was, though, he did want to do it again. And he wanted to be a part of Omega Place; he wanted to belong to something that mattered, that was bigger than him. Being with Terri and Rob was the front line, and he didn't think he'd ever felt quite so alive as he had high up that pole, giving two fingers to the authoritarian sods and their cameras: their evil eyes, as Terri called them.

'Rob?'

'Yeah?'

'When d'you think Terri's gonna tell, y'know, Orlando, that you've like got me in tow?'

'Dunno. Ask her, man, not me.'

'Why's it up to her?'

'Cos it's not my stupid idea, man.'

Right. Still a waste a space, then. Paul tried to shake off the negative vibe.

'What d'you think he's gonna say?'

'Orlando?'

Paul nodded.

'Anyone's guess . . . he'll probably ask Sky what he thinks, as that's who you'll be working with.'

'How comes you aren't working with Sky, if he's the one found you?'

'What's Terri been blabbing, man?'

'She's not blabbed nothing, Rob, just said it was at Glastonbury where you met Sky, that's all.'

'And?' Rob had turned sideways on the seat, leaning back against the window, and was looking questioningly at Paul. Hard eyes.

'And nothing . . . just, like, said he'd caught you stealing. Said you were good at it, but he was better at spotting you at it.'

Rob's face broke into a wide grin. 'Well, that's true enough. Like my social worker said, if there's one thing a Gillespie's good at it's nicking! Prob'ly said it was the *only* thing. Can't argue with that . . .'

Apart from the van and a mobile phone, Paul had also

witnessed Rob lifting a couple of books and a wallet so far on their journey south. The wallet was for petrol money, Rob had said. Just the cash, as the credit cards were worthless without their chip 'n' pin numbers, though according to Rob a fair few people kept them in their wallets, which was handy. He was a total pirate. Completely fearless, but careful, he lifted anything and everything he could lay his hands on, just because he could get away with it. Terri had said he almost never came out of a motorway service station without *something*, even if, like the books, he didn't want them as he couldn't read. And unless he was asleep, Paul had also discovered, Rob pretty much didn't stop talking.

'. . . still, if you're good at something, you should work at it, right? I remember them saying that at school, when I could be bothered to go.'

'Bothered?' Paul frowned. 'Didn't your mam make you?'

'Her? They took us away from me mam when I was five or so, put me in care and tried to get people to take us for the next ten years. I think I had more foster parents on my file than bloody social workers. And I had a fair few of those, man.'

'Where was your dad all this time?'

Rob shrugged, letting loose a small, humourless laugh. 'Me dad was the Invisible Man, Pauly. I never saw him. Never once, that I can remember. And me mam was a bit of an alky, couldn't cope with the four of us. I took off when I was, like, you know, mebbe twenty . . . left Carlisle and I've not been back since.'

Paul didn't know what to say. However shitty he'd thought his own life had been since his parents split, it paled into insignificance beside the crap Rob had had to deal with. He felt kind of embarrassed – even if Rob was a liar and only half the story was true – for even thinking he'd had a hard time.

'Why'd you get out, man?' Rob opened the glove compartment and took a Twix from the stash. 'Want one?'

'No, thanks.' He thought about why he'd left home. His nice, comfortable house with a mam who would do anything for him . . . and a stepfather he didn't get on with. Didn't sound like such a bad place to be. Paul glanced at Rob as he took one of the bars out, broke it in half and put the lot in his mouth; no wonder he had spots, and such shitty teeth. Unlike his, what with his mam being paranoid about taking him to the bloody dentist it seemed like all the time.

'So, Pauly, what's your story, morning glory?'

'Me? I'd had it with me stepdad, basically . . .'

'He take his belt to you?'

Paul shook his head. No, Rob, he thought, he tried to make me like him with too many expensive gifts and never laid a finger on me; he just wasn't me real dad, and he never will be.

Down the road Paul saw the bright lights of a sign for a service station.

'I'll stop at this next place, shall I?'

Rob had closed his eyes, catnapping again. 'Why not, man. One's as good as another . . . what is it?'

'Howd'you mean, what is it?'

'You know, like what kind of petrol?'

'Dunno, why?'

Rob sat up and grinned, rummaging in the pocket of his hoodie. 'Hope it's a Texaco, man! There was a voucher in that wallet I got, five quid or something . . . we'll get some more sweets, right?'

They'd finally made the outskirts of Birmingham. Over halfway to London. Paul sat behind the wheel of the van, watching Rob walk away down the street with Terri. This gig, she'd said, didn't need more than the regulation two people. And anyway, he'd done most of the driving, he could take a rest.

They'd trawled the city, looking for a good target, and then parked up in a place that was low traffic and well off-camera. There was no way they could get in or out of the city centre without being tracked – something, Terri said, that was true of most towns and cities. But what they need-ed was somewhere they could leave the van where they wouldn't be caught on film and connected with it, even if it was going to be ditched for something else before they got back to London. Change transport like you change your socks. Another of Orlando's rules, apparently.

So here he was, sat on his own in a deserted, badly-lit side street in some place called Erdington. Him, a mobile and more chocolate bars than his local corner shop. Bored. Nothing to do. And he'd been told to stay put, that he'd get a call that they were on their way back from doing the job and he should be ready to pick them up.

Lying across the front bench seat – the most comfortable place in the van, even though he couldn't fully stretch out – Paul wondered whether this was another of their tests. To see if he'd follow orders. More than likely it was, so he wasn't going to go anywhere. And he was tired, aching from sitting on his arse for hours, so maybe a kip wouldn't be such a bad thing. He made sure the volume on the mobile was up high, the vibrate turned on, and pulled his hood round his head. If his friend Dave could see him now, he thought as he closed his eyes.

He had no idea how long he'd been asleep, and for a moment couldn't work out why he'd woken up. The mobile wasn't ringing . . . and then he heard voices. Two people . . . but it wasn't Terri and Rob. It sounded like the people were whispering and he wondered why. Did whoever it was know he was in the van?

And then the thought didn't so much occur to him as land with a thud in his head as he stared at the roof. Police.

Had they spotted that the van and its plates weren't a match? And if they were the police, what was he supposed to do now? What was Orlando's rule for this situation? Make a run for it?

Paul lay still, hardly breathing, straining to hear what was going on outside on the street. As he waited, right near the passenger side of the van, where his head was, someone spoke.

'Reckon it's alarmed, Stewie?'

'Reckon not. Ain't that flash, is it? Try the bleedin' door and see, eh?'

So, not the cops . . . and then another thought occurred to him. Had he remembered to lock the doors? For the life of him he couldn't remember. More than likely not, knowing him.

'What d'you reckon's in it, like?'

'How the hell should *I* know?'

'Just askin', no need to get your knickers in a twist, OK?'

'Just try the door, OK? Then I'll see if I can jemmy the back, see what's in there.'

Dominant in the confused mess of thoughts and emotions that his head was trying to sort into a coherent plan was the fact that all he had going for him was the element of surprise. Which he'd lose the moment the door was opened or he was spotted. If he didn't do something, right now, it was going to be too late.

Paul gave himself a short, three-two-one countdown, sat bolt upright, swinging round to face the window as he did so, and screamed, eyes wide, teeth bared. Screamed like a murderous, bloodthirsty banshee. One that was about to burst out of the van.

The other side of the glass the shadowy figure of a skinny, skanky-looking bloke in a dark-coloured puffa jacket squealed like a girl who'd seen a mouse, and then cannoned into his friend as he leapt backwards, both of them landing on the pavement in a heap of arms and legs and swearing.

Paul was so wired and strung out that it was only later, as he told Terri and Rob what had happened, that he was able to see the funny side of the story. Right in the middle of it, heart pounding, all he wanted to do was get away and he pushed himself over into the driving seat, fumbled the screwdriver 'key' into the busted ignition, revved the engine, slammed the gearstick forward and dropped the clutch.

As the van screeched off down the street, the mobile started to ring. The mobile that was the other side of the bench seat.

It could only be Terri or Rob.

He had to answer it. Right now.

Paul slammed on the brakes, somehow remembering to drop the box into neutral so he didn't stall, and leaned across to grab the phone.

As he reached over, Paul saw in the van's offside mirror

the two would-be thieves literally fall over themselves in their efforts to run away. Looked like they reckoned he was a homicidal maniac about to reverse back to get them, he thought as he picked up the call.

'Uh . . . yeah?'

'Pauly?'

'Yeah?' Still breathless.

'Where were you, man? You been out for a run?'

'No . . . no, just forgot which pocket I'd put the phone in. Sorry.'

'Safe. We're ready. Swing by that roundabout, OK? We'll be there in a couple of minutes, so take it nice and easy.'

'No problem.' Paul cut the call, his hands shaking ever so slightly. Right. Nice and easy. He was going to drive like a bloody granny.

10

Monday 31st July, Thames House

Jane Mercer sat at her desk. As she worked through her list of Current Files she thought about what the director had told her when she'd been called to his office late on Friday, and wondered just how much of a poisoned chalice this job was going to turn out to be. Was it going to end up being a dubious privilege? You really did have to be more than a little bit paranoid to work in this place, but while it was a good idea to be unreasonably suspicious and mistrustful of the people you were investigating, was it quite so healthy to feel the same way about the people you were working with and for?

Was she being set up for a fall? Given the job no one else wanted because it was a sod of a job, with little chance of success? Who wanted that on their record? All she could do was do her best, tough it out.

Mercer glanced at the rest of the files that had been sent over to her by the Threat Evaluation team. She picked up one of the stack of buff-coloured folders. It was ominously stamped 'FYEO' in red on the cover, but with initials in the tracking box that showed it had been read by a number of other people and wasn't really for her eyes only at all. She opened the folder and reread the Home Office document that was on top.

In essence, it said that the country's CCTV network was the envy of the policed world and long may it remain so.

Whatever the critics argued – and there were plenty of them – the document continued, the general public had clearly bought into the idea of the benevolent watchers, bought in big time, and no one in any position of responsibility wanted this situation to change. As with so much to do with government, it was all about the status quo. Changes, especially when they came from outside, were never a good thing.

Mercer knew the statistics in the Omega Place leaflet were accurate and that there really was one camera for every fourteen people in the country, give or take, and over a quarter of a million of them in London alone. The figures were actually quite extraordinary as they meant that tabs could be kept on a hell of a lot of people, in a hell of a lot of places. George Orwell must be looking down, nodding sagely and saying to himself, 'I told you so. I just got the year wrong . . .', as the public at large didn't appear to mind the CCTV network. Perceived wisdom said it made them feel safe, and that any thoughts they might have about 'Big Brother' made them think of some inane TV reality show, not a highly organised invasion of their privacy.

Flicking through the papers, Mercer wondered about Omega Place. The files told her next to nothing about them, because sod all was precisely what they knew. She sat back and looked up at the random patterns in the ceiling tiles above her, trying to visualise what her next moves should be. Just like the patterns, there was nothing immediately obvious.

In terms of 'threat to the nation', Omega Place figured about as high up the list as the Boy Scouts. If all they were doing was putting a few CCTV cameras out of action – some of which probably weren't even operational anyway – then this would all be a proverbial storm in a teacup. But, as Markham had very pointedly made clear, it wasn't what they were *doing* that had got the Home Secretary so worked up, it was what they were *saying*, which was where the TOP SECRET document in the folder came into play.

She turned over pages until she found it, and scanned the first few paragraphs. If the general public became aware of the facts behind the government's Remotely Piloted Aircraft Programme they might not be as laid back about it as they were about the proliferation of static CCTV cameras. Tiny RPAs – basically, remotely controlled spy planes equipped with all kinds of cameras, which had been successfully road tested in Iraq and Afghanistan – were apparently now undergoing classified trials in urban situations here at home. Eyes in the sky: small enough, quiet enough and manoeuvrable enough to go anywhere. Quite frightening, really. If you were 'them' and not 'us'. It all depended, she supposed, on whether you trusted the people in charge. Trusted them not to misuse their power.

Mercer, who liked to believe she was on the side of the angels, picked up a ballpoint cap and began chewing on it. The fact was, even she wasn't supposed to know about this, let alone a bunch of misanthropes with anti-establishment tendencies who were littering the streets with the news in their so-called Manifesto 3. The only positive thing was that, so far, the press hadn't picked up the story, but surely it wouldn't be long before they did.

So, to put it simply, what she had to do was (1) stop this Omega Place lot from disseminating any more highly classified information, and (2) find out how the hell they got hold of said info in the first place, and then (3) close

71

the bastards down.

The reason she was feeling so nervous and antsy was because this knowledge was black. It didn't exist, outside of certain very secure walls. She chewed harder on the pen cap. Someone pretty high up the ladder had either screwed up or gone bad. And it was her job to find out who that person was. But no one liked internal investigations. Or the investigators. Her future, she knew, depended on finding the right person (failure wasn't good for career prospects) and it also depended on who it turned out to be. The wrong kind of 'right person' could mean no career prospects for her at all.

Like the jokers always said, just because you were paranoid didn't mean they weren't after you.

Mercer had almost finished going through the first two files when her computer *dinged* to let her know she'd just received an email. She stopped reading and opened it to find a message from someone in Oversight, otherwise known as Eavesdroppers Inc., the electronic surveillance department. This someone, who signed off as C. Farmer, was passing on, as requested by S. Pearce in Threat Evaluation, 'all the information so far gathered'. Mercer scrolled down, attempting to discover what information had been gathered about whom, and found an attached document.

Dragging it on to her desktop, she made a mental note to read it just as soon as she'd finished going through everything else that was on the desk in front of her. She had to have everything ready for an early start tomorrow. The first day of the rest of her life . . .

*   *   *

72

Henry Garden looked at the printout he'd brought with him from home. He'd deleted the original email before shutting down his computer and coming to work, and would shred this paper in a minute or two. He'd spent the weekend waiting for some communication from Nick – no call to his mobile or landline, no email. Nothing. Until this morning. And now this. Not what you wanted to read first thing on a Monday morning. Quite how he'd managed not to buy a packet of fags over the last two days, he did not know. He scanned the email again and felt his gut tighten, like it did just before he made a bet . . .

Subject: Contact

Date: Monday 31 July, 2006 7.46 a.m.

From: N. J. H. <Jerez@btinternet.com>

To: Henry Garden <geegee62@onetel.net>

Got yr message, Friday p.m. Be at St Martin's Lane box, 7.00 p.m. tonight.

Something was wrong.

It had to be when the only secure way to get in touch was through a public phone booth in St Martin's Lane. But what the hell was it? Today was going to be a bloody nightmare. He could already feel the tension building up in his neck; just one long wait until he could go home, with one single thought on his mind: exactly how much of the mud that was more than likely about to be flung was going to come his way?

Garden leaned over and fed the printout into the piranha teeth of his shredder, listening to them shriek as it ate the paper and spat the bits into the bin below. He sat for a moment, then got up, took the strands of paper out of the otherwise empty bin, tore them in half as he walked over to the blue recycling bin and dropped them in. You could never be too careful. Ever.

11

Monday 31st July, M1 southbound

Another day, another van. A Merc this time, taken the night before from a motorway service station car park. Rob seemed to treat these places as his personal rental company – drop off, pick up, no charge, no mileage. For all that he was some kind of a one-man crime wave, Paul had to admit that Rob was genuinely impressive to watch at work. And he took his work very seriously – if they caught you because you were lazy and slack, you only got what you deserved, he said. And because he could sometimes act like such an obnoxious chancer, it had been weird to discover that he didn't take any unnecessary risks, like he insisted everyone always drove pretty much within speed limits. Nice and easy, monkey don't get catchee, he said.

Last night they'd tried three car parks before Rob was satisfied everything was right. He'd chosen the Merc van because it had newish tyres for its age and seemed reasonably well looked after. It was also parked behind a larger truck, obscuring it from view from the shop and cafe while he broke in and they changed the plates, using one of the fake sets, backed with industrial-strength, double-sided sticky tape they had with them. The transfer of ownership had taken minutes and then they were off again. London bound.

And now here they were, according to the last sign, with just thirty miles to go before they'd be there. Paul glanced across at Terri, taking her turn in the driving seat.

'Have you told Orlando, Terri?'

'Told him what?'

Rob, his feet up on the dashboard, was drumming along to some track on the radio. 'Poor old Pauly's getting twitchy, sis . . . put him out of his misery, eh?'

'No, I haven't spoken to him, Pauly, cos he's not called me . . . and we don't call him, remember, Rob? Security, right?' Terri indicated, pulled out and overtook a loaded car transporter in the middle lane. 'You'll just have to wait. We're all gonna have to wait at the next service area anyway, if he hasn't called before then.'

Rob stopped drumming on his legs. 'Why?'

'Cos the squat was raided. They had to move to a new place, and we don't know where it is.'

'Shit! When did *that* happen? You never said a bloody word!'

'Didn't I?'

'Don't try and bullshit a bullshitter, man – when did you find out? Did Or-bloody-*lando* tell you not to say anything to me, or what? Didn't youse two trust me?'

'No, he never said not to tell you, Rob, OK? All I got was a text, no details, and I forgot, right? Sorr-ee . . .' Terri rammed the gear stick up into fifth and started to accelerate. 'What would you have done if I *had* remembered to tell you? You never liked the stupid place anyway, always moaning that the sodding room you were in was too small.'

'Slow down. You're going eighty.'

'Piss off.'

Paul could feel the van was still accelerating as Terri moved into the fast lane. If he leaned back, the speedometer was just about visible, and as the needle crept round the dial the tension in the van was ramping up with it. How fast was she going now – ninety? Ninety-five? Terri was only doing it to wind Rob up, but that wasn't such a cool thing to do right here, right now. This was like when his parents had been falling apart, just before the divorce, and every drive had been a murderous experience. He'd sit in the back of the car, desperate for them to stop nagging and bitching at each other and feeling that it – whatever the 'it' was they were arguing about – was all his fault, that if he'd not ever been there they'd somehow be OK with each other.

The three of them stuck here in this claustrophobic space for hours and hours on end was enough to drive anyone gaga without the added stress of a crap argument, but what was he supposed to do? Paul stole a look to his right: Terri, gripping the wheel like she was fighting it, staring straight ahead, speedo approaching launch velocity, ferchrissake! To his left Rob had leaned forward, one hand on the dash, and was eyeballing Terri with a homicidal stare. Great. Mexican stand-off.

Which was when he saw a sign.

It said London Gateway Services, next exit. This had to be the one Terri was talking about. And then, up ahead, he saw the sign with the three diagonal white stripes on a blue background, which meant the exit was coming up and they were still rocketing down the fast lane. Now or never . . .

'Is this where we have to wait?'

'What?' Terri almost barked.

'London Gateway . . . is this where we have to wait for that call from, you know, Orlando?'

'Christ!'

Terri went all flight-deck commander – braking, checking her mirrors, indicating left, dropping a gear, then another –

as she scythed the van across two motorway lanes towards the fast-approaching exit slip road, just making it as the sound of some pissed-off driver's horn faded away down the motorway. As she slowed the van to thirty, coasting round on to the road that would take them over the carriageway below and through into the service area, Paul stopped pressing hard on the imaginary brake pedal and relaxed a bit.

No one said a word as Terri drove across the car park and found a space close to the exit back on to the motorway. When she finally stopped she pulled up the handbrake, switched off the engine, sat back and started rolling a cigarette. Still nothing. Paul sat there, piggy-in-the-middle, remembering that often, with his parents, the silences had been worse than the arguments. Cold, empty spaces; vacuums lined with razor blades . . . enter at your peril. At least if people were talking – even shouting – at each other there was a chance they'd sort shit out.

Paul had no idea why he said it, but the words 'Are we there yet?' just kind of escaped from his brain and out of his mouth in a childish whine. The pressure bubble burst and all three of them were cackling like hyenas on laughing gas, Terri banging the steering wheel with her fist, Rob stumbling out of the cabin, tears running down his cheeks and claiming he was about to piss himself.

As he held on to his aching sides, Paul wondered why it had never been that easy with his parents.

Rob swung the van into the multi-storey car park Orlando had told them to go to when he'd finally rung up. He pulled up and took the ticket the automatic machine stuck out like a tongue.

'Where did he say? Top floor?'

Terri nodded. 'Yeah. They'll be in a red Almera, he said.'

'Saloon?'

'*I* don't know!' Terri shook her head.

'Prob'ly is . . . he doesn't like estates. Who's with him?'

'Sky, who else?'

Rob dropped a gear and slowed for the tight bend that would take them on to the ramp to the first floor. 'So where is the new place?'

'He wouldn't say.'

'Why?'

'Security, Rob.' Terri nudged Paul in the ribs. 'Got to check the newbie out first, right?'

Paul sat looking straight ahead. What the hell was he doing, letting himself be put through this shit? Did he really need this? Right from the moment Terri had finished the call from Orlando and told him and Rob what the plan was, right from then he could have walked. They'd been having coffee at the service area when her mobile had finally gone. The moment he'd found out about this crap 'security meeting' (in a bloody multi-storey car park ferchrissake, like some cop show!) he could have got up from the table, taken his stuff from the van and gone off to look for another lift.

They mightn't have let him, but he didn't even try.

He *could've* told Terri to let him out when Rob had stopped to get the ticket for this place – his last chance to make a move.

But he didn't.

He'd stayed put and not said a peep and now he was being driven up to the top of this shopping-mall car park to be checked out. Given the once-over by Orlando and Sky,

79

who both sounded like characters from some dumb, kids' Saturday morning TV show . . . a stripy orange fuzzy blob and a blue one, each with silly voices. Why hadn't he asked more questions? What if these people actually were seriously deranged?

Rob accelerated up the final ramp, paused at the top and turned right.

'Red Almera, was it?'

'Yeah.'

'I'll do a go-round. Keep your eyes peeled.'

Paul coughed and cleared his throat. 'What happens if they, like, say no?'

Rob winked at him. 'Sky shoots you. Single bullet in the back of the head, man. SS-style.'

'It's SAS, you berk . . .' Terri turned from her car search. 'And if they decide it's a "no", you've had a totally unique free ride down to London and you walk away. Simple as that. That's why we're doing this, so's you don't know anything important, right?'

'There it is, Terri, over in the corner.'

Paul looked where Rob was pointing and saw a red saloon in the shadows. Then its headlights flashed once. This was it.

Rob flicked the beam control to return the signal. 'I'll park this up; there was a space just on the other side.'

As they drove past the red car Paul could see the silhouettes of two people inside. Neither moved.

'Get everything of yours out the back, OK, Paul?' Terri undid her seat belt. 'Whatever happens, we're leaving the van here.'

Then her mobile started to ring.

*   *   *

80

Paul sat alone in the Merc. Again. Terri and Rob had taken their bags and stuff to go and talk to Orlando, which was what the phone call had been about. Leave him to stew while they talk about him behind his back. Tense, he fiddled with his Celtic-style ring. He looked at his backpack, sitting next to him on the seat, and wondered why he wasn't taking this last opportunity to walk away. What was it about this whole thing that had so got under his skin?

Was it that he felt kind of more alive than he ever had? That he wanted *more* of the adrenalin rush, *more* of the freedom and the gypsy life? Even though, if they did take him in, he wouldn't be actually spending that much time with Terri. Because, best be honest with himself, she was another reason why staying was more of an option than going. Not that he'd got a chance of getting anywhere with her. Well out of his range. But he'd never know for sure if he didn't stay, would he?

So here he was in London, possibly at the start of something, maybe not. The main thing was he *wasn't* still up in Newcastle. His mam always talked about the times she'd visited, and now he'd made it. Paul got his phone out . . . he wouldn't tell her where he was . . . just that he was OK. After sending the text he thought about sending another one to Dave, just so's someone else would know he'd done it, broken away, come south, even if it was only for a few weeks. But he didn't. Just being here wasn't enough, he wanted to be able to tell Dave he had a job – any bloody job would do – and a place to live. That he was doing all right.

Lost in his daydream he didn't see the bloke get out of the Almera. Paul only noticed him when he was walking up to the van. He was quite tall, with straggly, greying hair and a grey moustache, dressed in what looked like black Reeboks, jeans, a check shirt over a white T-shirt and a dark grey denim jacket. It wasn't until he got closer that he saw the man wasn't as young as he looked, that, from the lines on his face, he was probably quite old. Paul guessed probably older than his dad . . . in his late forties, something like that. It was hard to tell exactly.

Watching the man approach the passenger side of the van he wondered if this was Orlando or if it was Sky, figuring, from what little Rob and Terri had said, that it was probably Sky, Orlando apparently being the background type. This time he'd locked the doors, so when the man tried to open the van he had to wait for Paul to reach over and let him in. Sitting back behind the wheel, Paul left his rucksack on the seat, like a demarcation line – my side, your side – and watched the man climb in and close the door.

He looked over at Paul, eyeing him up and down. 'Paul, right?' Slow, soft American accent, like wood that had been sanded down and polished.

It was Sky.

Paul nodded. 'Yeah. And you must be, um, you must be Sky.'

The radio was on. Green Day's 'Boulevard of Broken Dreams'. Neither of them spoke, almost like they were both listening to the music, waiting for the track to finish.

Sky took a small tin out of his jacket pocket and Paul saw that there was a packet of liquorice papers and some hand-rolling tobacco inside.

'You smoke, Paul?'

'No.'

'Sensible. Wish I didn't.' Sky held up the cigarette he'd made. 'You mind?'

'Go ahead.' Paul opened the window next to him an inch or two.

Sky wound down his window a bit, then took out a bronze Zippo, flicked it open and lit the cigarette. He inhaled, blowing a stream of smoke out of the van. Paul watched and waited. Everything the man did seemed to be measured, calculated, unhurried, done to his own personal timescale.

'You weren't ticked off at being kidnapped?'

The question wasn't what he'd been expecting – he'd been *expecting* something like 'Why d'you want in with Omega Place?' It took Paul by surprise. He started to answer, then stopped for a moment to think to remember how he had felt at the time. 'Yeah . . . to begin with, I was pretty pissed off. Scared the shit out of me.'

'And then?'

'Realised I must've looked suspicious, following Terri.'

'You'd seen them before.' A statement, not a question.

'Yeah, in Graingertown.'

'That was careless of them.' Sky tapped ash out of the window.

'Not really. I was right in the back of a doorway, covered by a cardboard box. No way they'd have seen me.'

'So it was just one of those rare, rare things, like a totally pure coincidence, that you saw them again?'

Paul studied the man, staring at his face, searching his pale brown eyes, looking for some kind of sign as to what was going on in his head. Did this Sky bloke really think that he was up to something? He wondered what Terri and Rob had said . . . surely they must've talked him up, otherwise why bother to bring him this far? Paul looked over at the red car. Had his fate already been decided, and was Sky just playing with him before delivering the message?

'You can believe what you like, mate. You and Orlando.' Paul nodded at the Almera. 'They trusted me, and I never let them down. I proved myself. Ask them.'

'I did. But why should *I* trust you, guy?' The Zippo came out and was flicked into life again. 'Why should I put *my* neck on the line on their say-so? See my point of view? Entirely selfish, I know, but that's how I got this far. Doing it my way.'

'You think I'll let you down, or you think I'd, like, go to the cops? Is that it?'

'Maybe you don't know . . . they didn't tell you . . . but I've been on the outside a *very* long time. Like more than thirty-five years. Since I was nineteen and went over the border into Canada, rather than go and fight in that bullshit war in Vietnam.' Sky saw Paul's frown and smiled slowly. 'Yeah, I really am as old as I look . . . and there's a part of me, the leery, suspicious and goddam paranoid part of me, that's kept my bones safe all these years. And it doesn't believe in coincidences and the right people turning up at just the right time. Like you, my friend . . . just like you.'

Paul waited, expecting the axe to fall, but Sky looked away and didn't say anything. Was that it? What was he supposed to do – just walk off? Not him.

'You could give me a chance, couldn't you? Someone must've given you a chance once, let you prove them wrong. Why not me?'

Sky narrowed his eyes, fine lines radiating out across the side of his face in a fan, and smoothed his moustache with his right hand. The very picture of a man thinking hard. Was he taking the piss? Paul didn't know him well enough to know.

'In a strange kinda way . . .' Sky turned to look at Paul, '. . . in a *strange* way you kinda remind me of me at your age. I was in Washington D.C. then, burning my draft card – a war *resister*, not some chickenshit draft dodger, or some dumbass boy with a rich daddy, like George W. We had something to protest about back then, because they wanted to take the ultimate freedom away from us, sending us to die in the jungles . . .'

Another silence, during which Paul wondered what the hell all this stuff that happened a couple of lifetimes ago had to do with him now, and the DJ started playing an Oasis track.

'Why d'you want to come in with us? You want to change things, mess with the status quo?'

'Me?' Another surprise question. What was the right answer? How the hell was he supposed to know, and did he care? As Paul sat back and looked out of the van, something his dad had often told him, a quote he'd seen in some magazine and cut out, came back to him. Any fool can tell the truth, it said, but it takes a clever man to lie well. What was the honest truth about why he wanted in? Paul looked back at Sky.

'I dunno about changing things . . . I liked what it said in the Manifesto. I did good, you know, up in Leeds and stuff, it was a blast. And I need somewhere to stay.'

Sky made another thinking face as he nodded to himself. 'And Terri is quite cute, which is another way of looking at it.' He rolled up his window and opened the door. 'Get your bag.'

'What?'

'I'm giving you a chance.'

85

12

Monday 31st July, St Martin's Lane, London

Nick was late. Henry Garden had got to the phone booth at around five to seven and had been hanging round like some sad, lovelorn teenager, waiting for the phone to ring, ever since. About five minutes ago it had occurred to him that he'd either got the time or the place wrong, but, as he'd shredded the email printout, there was no way of checking for sure.

As the seconds built steadily into minutes, the temptation to cross the road and buy a packet of cigarettes and a disposable lighter was pretty intense. But he didn't dare move. Not because he didn't want to give way to the little devil on his shoulder but just in case the call did, finally, come through while he was away. If he didn't pick up PDQ, Nick would give him a load of crap, and after the day he'd had that was the last thing he wanted. Really.

It was almost a quarter past seven when the phone rang. Garden pulled the booth's door open and almost pounced on the receiver. It was, he registered as he picked it up, unpleasantly tacky. With the door closed the confined space smelled like an ashtray, which, looking at the ground, was what it was. Garden's nostrils pricked and synapses snapped together in his brain as he breathed in deeply.

'Nick?'

'Yes.'

'You did say seven o'clock?'

'I was delayed. Unavoidably.'

The day Nicholas Harvey apologised, thought Garden as he took a paper handkerchief from the packet in his suit pocket and wrapped it round the receiver, would be the day you could ice-skate in hell.

'You got my message on Friday, then, Nick?'

'I did.'

'I thought I might hear from you over the weekend.'

'Well, you thought wrong, sunshine. I had a bit of electronic housekeeping to do . . . covering my tracks, so to speak.'

'It's serious, then?'

'You bet your life, Henry old son . . .'

There was a pause, one of those almost-silences in which all you could really hear was static. Like when someone puts their hand over the mouthpiece to talk about you.

'Nick? Are you there?'

'Yeah, sure. Look, tell me what happened on Friday, and what's happened since, Henry. All the detail.'

'Not a lot to add to what I said on Friday, except that I gather Markham has set in motion this taskforce. Put some junior officer in charge, so may not be taking the whole thing as seriously as he might. That's the scuttlebutt, anyway. But, as you might imagine, I'm keeping as clear of all this as I can.'

'Don't get too far away from events. I need to be kept in the loop on this one, Henry . . . right in the loop. And I'm relying on you like never before, OK? So just exactly how *did* they find out about Omega Place?'

Garden's eyes were drawn to the blanket of tart cards Blu-tacked to the wall in front of him, his concentration momentarily distracted by the display of flesh. He looked away.

'Someone found some flyers or leaflets and stickers during a raid on a squat, apparently. It was the mention of the RPAs that set the cat among the pigeons.'

'I'll bet.'

'I thought "Omega Place" was just a code name, Nick. Not real, not an actual *thing*.'

'True enough, Henry, that's what it was supposed to be. Originally. Shit happens, though . . . isn't that what they say?'

Jane Mercer looked up from the document she was reading as the door to her office opened and Ray Salter, her second-in-command, came in. She watched him pull out a chair and sit down.

'Wild goose well and truly chased, boss.'

'Translation?'

'You asked me to look into the name, Omega Place?'

Mercer nodded.

'Well, it turns up in a grand total of twenty-three locations throughout mainland UK. From West Lothian in the north to Tiverton in the south and *lots* of places in between.'

'Anything in London?'

'Yup.' Salter flicked through the file he was carrying, pulled out a sheet of paper and slid it across the desk. 'A tiny little cul de sac at the bottom of the Caledonian Road, the scuzzy end. It's ringed in red, for ease of location . . .'

Ignoring the comment, Mercer examined the printout of the map. 'You been to take a look at it yet?'

Salter shook his head. 'Not yet, boss.'

Mercer sat back, pointing at the file. 'You leaving that for me?'

'With pleasure.' Salter put the file on the desk and stood up.

'Have you started looking into James Baker's past?'

'All I've got so far is in there with whatever the Threat Evaluation lot gave us.' Salter nodded at the file. 'Basically, the only extra thing I managed to add to it, apart from some stuff from when he was at Birmingham, was his birth certificate. Or at least a copy of it. His middle name's Hudson . . . James Hudson Baker.'

Mercer reached over for the file. 'And nothing to show that James *Hudson* Baker ever lived anywhere called Omega Place?'

'No such luck, boss.'

'OK, see you in our new accommodation tomorrow.'

'How many others have we got?' Salter stopped at the door.

'Two, John Perry and Tony Castleton.'

'Very generous.'

'Inordinately.' Mercer sat back in her chair. 'We are going to have our work cut out for us.'

'Don't stay too late, boss.'

As the door closed behind Salter, Mercer rifled through the file until she came across the birth certificate; opening it out she saw that James Baker's mother's maiden name had been Hudson, which explained that. A couple of pages later she found a reference to the fact that both Mr and Mrs Baker were deceased and that James had been an only child. So the family wasn't going to be much help.

Tidying up the papers and closing the file, Mercer wondered what and who James Baker was. Because, whoever he turned out to be, he'd somehow managed to get hold of some highly classified material and thereby yanked the chain of some people with very short tempers. Real Rottweilers. Unfortunately for James, because his were the only prints that had been found and identified, he was the one everybody now had in their sights. And when they caught him, which they probably would, life was going to get fairly unpleasant.

13

Monday 31st July, Kingsland Road, east London

Sky turned the car off a main road and into a nondescript street, like almost every other one they'd driven down since they'd left the car park, and Paul still had no idea where he was. Sat in the back, with Rob and Terri, he'd tried to take in his surroundings, get to grips with the concept that he was actually *in* London – more accurately, driving through some drab bit of it – but he was finding it difficult.

All he'd seen since they'd left the M1 was mile after mile of the monotonous, low-rise housing and strips of shops that lined the roads. Roads, it seemed, that were filled with a stop-start blanket of cars. He'd seen nothing that looked so very different from home and he didn't want to appear naive by asking too many questions about where they were. Certainly not in front of Rob, although he'd now fallen asleep, head lolling forward like someone had taken the bones out of his neck. He seemed to be able to catch a nap whenever the opportunity arose. Another of his odd talents.

Paul was sitting behind Sky, who whistled through his teeth as he drove, but throughout the journey he'd kept looking out of the corner of his eye at the man in the passenger seat. Orlando. He'd hardly said a word to anyone since Paul had got in the car and been introduced – and that had only been a mumbled hello, a nod as he looked him over and not a lot else. What was *his* problem?

Not that it was easy to tell when he was sitting down, but Orlando didn't give the impression of being a tall person; maybe that was his problem. He certainly didn't look like much, with his narrow, slightly dandruff-specked shoulders and untidy, brown hair (thinning on top, it looked like). And he wore glasses, wire-rimmed. Hard to say how old he was.

But while he didn't look like much, not even kind of rugged, like Sky, there was something about him. He had that way about him that some teachers did, broadcasting his mood, 'radiating the vibe', like Dave said, and dominating not through in-your-face aggression, but the threat of what he might do or say. Mr Sanders – the Napoleon of the science wing – had been like that. Sarky bastard.

The car pulled up. 'We're here, boys and girls . . .' Sky cut the engine, got out and opened Paul's door. 'Be it ever so simple,' he pointed with his chin at the terraced house they were parked opposite, 'there's no place like home.'

Paul looked at the place, taking in the small, overgrown front garden, weather-beaten paintwork and general air of shabbiness. It didn't look like home to him.

Orlando had disappeared upstairs the moment they'd got in the house, leaving Sky to introduce Paul to Izzy Morley and Tommy Walsh, the final pieces of the puzzle. And it was awkward, weird to be standing there with his backpack, the stranger coming in from the outside. An unknown quantity, there to replace a friend who had died.

This is Paul, guys . . . he's the new Jez.

Sky hadn't actually said that, but that was how it felt.

Rob yawned and slumped into a chair at the kitchen table. 'We found him in Newcastle,' he said to no one in particular, as if that explained everything.

'Is he any good?' This from Tommy, shaven-headed Tommy, who was sitting perched on the work surface, cradling a mug of tea, a wide, innocent-looking smile beaming out from his pale, freckled face. Below which, Paul noticed, hung a small gold crucifix on a chain.

Izzy – small, dark-haired, intense, standing by the cooker, looking spiky – took a drag from her cigarette. 'Are you the new Jez, then, Paul? That's gonna be one hard act to follow.'

'No, I'm not . . .'

Sky moved into the room and sat at the table. 'He's cool, Izzy, and he's not the new anyone. Why should he be?'

'Dead man's shoes.'

'Leave it out, Izzy, OK?' Terri checked the kettle, then filled it at the sink.

Sky started to roll a cigarette. 'Terri and Rob put him through his paces . . . they say he's fine, so that's fine by me.'

Tommy slid off the work surface. 'He in with me 'n' Rob?'

'Yeah.' Sky nodded.

Paul, standing at the door to the kitchen, not quite in, not quite out, watched the proceedings with a feeling of dream-like detachment, like this was all some TV soap and not actually happening to him. Although he was the one who'd asked to be a part of what these people were doing, *they'd* said he could tag along and now *they* were making other decisions for him. Which wasn't quite what he'd been look-ing for in joining Omega Place.

'Want to take your stuff upstairs, mate?'

Paul realised Tommy was looking at him. 'Me?' He pointed to himself, immediately feeling stupid.

Tommy grinned as he walked towards him. 'Yeah, mate, you . . . come on.'

Tommy had helped put up the camp bed that Paul was now lying in, a garish tartan blanket over his sleeping bag and a lumpy pillow stuffed under his head. He couldn't sleep, even though he was tired. Thoughts and feelings and questions were streaming through his mind like a torrent and all he could do was stare at the ceiling and hope that the flow would stop and they'd just go away.

What a weird, *fucking* weird day. Really.

He was in London, in a squat! He'd always imagined a squat would be a filthy, rat-infested place with plaster hanging off the walls and holes in the floor. Although this place was no way a palace, and nothing like the home he'd so recently left, it wasn't *that* bad. There was power and water and pretty much all the basics. If you called a TV a basic.

Eyes wide open, brain racing, he thought about the rest of the people in the house. He'd kind of got used to Rob on the way down to London (a quiet voice in the back of his head whispering that he'd *love* to get more used to Terri . . .) and Sky, for all that he was quite serious about stuff, and so much older, seemed easy enough to get along with. And what *wasn't* there to like about Tommy? He gave the impression he didn't give much of a shit about anything and would, as his dad liked to say, rather be laughing.

It was Izzy and Orlando he didn't get. The two of them looked like they could make it tough going, each in their own particular way.

Tommy had sort of made excuses for Izzy when he was showing Paul the room and the layout of the squat, saying he shouldn't mind her, she was just upset about Jez . . . that they were all close-knit, like a family. When someone dies in a family, it's hard, he'd said. Which was true, but it didn't mean you had to take it out on someone who'd had nothing to do with what had happened. Mind you, he hadn't seen her be especially friendly or nice to anyone else, either.

And then there was Orlando, who was another thing altogether. Paul shifted in the camp bed, attempting to get more comfortable, which he kind of knew was just not going to happen. Orlando was . . . odd. No other way of putting it. For a start, he looked like a geek, but came on like he was The Man. The Man With All The Answers. Paul had watched him when they'd eaten – lasagne, cooked by Sky, the first real food he'd eaten in days. He could still taste the spicy meat sauce.

Orlando, like Izzy, had an attitude, but his seemed to be deeper somehow, ingrained, like dirt that you couldn't scrub off. He was obviously younger than Sky, but Sky was the one taking orders – consulted, but not in charge. How did geeks get to take control, be the ones who made the rules, become the boss? Force of character, he supposed. And having people around them who did what they were told. That would certainly help.

Paul wasn't sure whether he was the kind of person who did what he was told. When it came to his stepfather the answer was a definite, absolute no, and he wondered how this was all going to work out. Lying here, in this room, the sounds of two people he hardly knew drifting through their hours of sleep and keeping him awake, he could feel this negative space in his gut, an uneasy emptiness that he knew from experience would climb slowly towards panic, if he let it.

What was he doing here, with these people?

Maybe he should just get up, collect his stuff and leave.

See if he really could make it by himself in London. Why did he need to be with this lot? It had been exciting to be with Rob and Terri on the way down here, doing shit and getting a real buzz from it. But now, in this house, with the whole group and everything, he wasn't so sure. What had Tommy said? It was like a family. Except it was nothing like his family. He didn't have brothers or sisters. He'd never had to deal with any of that, didn't, he realised, actually *know* how to deal with it. Or really want to.

As he was turning over again, and rearranging the lumps in his pillow, Paul stopped. He could do with taking a leak. God, he was never going to get to sleep at this rate. As quietly as he could, he unzipped his sleeping bag and carefully eased himself off the flimsy camp bed. Standing on the threadbare carpet in his jockeys and a T-shirt, staring through bleary eyes at the monochrome darkness, he wondered what was happening back at home in Newcastle: was his mam in a flap about him going off and not coming back? Or did she think he was just away with mates and not worried at all?

He could always phone to find out . . .

No. If he called, she'd only try to get him to come home, and in the middle of all the uncertainty, the one thing Paul was sure of was that he didn't want to go home. Not right now. He stepped over a pair of trainers and a pile of someone's clothes and slowly turned the handle on the door, pulling it open just enough for him to slip through. The door to the bathroom, a few feet across the landing, was wide open and the glow of a street lamp through the frosted glass cast a pale, diffused shaft of orange, like a pathway, across the carpet.

Tiptoeing over to the bathroom he stepped on to the cold

lino flooring, which sent an involuntary shiver down his back, and was about to push the door to when he heard a voice. Voices? No . . . sounded like just the one. Paul stopped. Had someone left a radio or the TV on? He checked his watch, which wasn't there as he'd taken it off. Who knew what the time was. He took a couple of steps back, frowning as he listened harder, straining to see if he could pick up more of what was being said. No, he couldn't, but he was sure it was an actual person he could hear talking and not the TV.

He started for the bathroom again, thinking that what he should be doing was taking a piss and getting back to bed, so he could try to go to sleep. But then he stopped, curiosity getting the better of him. This was like when he was a kid, when his parents were starting to seriously bitch with each other. To begin with they never used to argue in front of him, saving it for when he'd gone to bed. He used to lie there, the sound of their voices filtering up through the floor of his room from the kitchen below.

Just the sound, the tone, the anger. None of the words.

What exactly they might be was left to his overactive imagination, which worked out that what his parents must be talking about was him. Sometimes he'd creep out of bed and hug the shadows until he was at the top of the stairs, where he'd sit in a huddle, peering through the banisters at the kitchen door.

With the same sense of risk and guilt he'd felt all those years ago, Paul went to the top of the stairs and leaned forward slightly. There was, now his eyes had adjusted, a faint glow from downstairs, which he could see was coming from the thin strip of light escaping from under the kitchen door. Whoever was talking was in there. Without really thinking about it, Paul sat down, resting his chin on his knees and automatically reaching to play with the ring on his little finger. It wasn't there and for a second he panicked that he might've lost it, finally remembering he'd put it on the small bamboo table between his and Tommy's bed, along with his chain.

The sound of chair legs scraping on the floor and footsteps.

'No!' said the voice.

Orlando. Slightly muffled, but it was him.

'Look, you don't control me . . . Agreement? What *agreement*?'

A long pause.

'Did I sign anything? . . . Forget it, you can't make me stop. What we're doing is important and *needs* to be done – and done for the right reasons . . . the public good, not personal gain . . .'

A humourless laugh.

'You don't get it, do you? This is my gig now, not yours.'

Silence. A long one.

'Look, I don't need your money any more. This "joke organisation", as you call it, is self-financing now . . . yeah, that's what I said, self-financing, and it's none of your sodding business how. Not that it ever really was . . .'

Silence. More footsteps.

'Are you threatening me? . . . And just exactly how are you going to do that, might I ask? You don't know where we . . . Southgate? No . . . no we, ah, we weren't ever there . . .'

The chair legs scraping on the floor again.

'Must, um . . . must've been someone else.' Orlando cleared his throat, sounded uncertain for a moment. 'I don't care what you say, what stupid threats you make, we're not stopping . . .'

A dull slap . . . Orlando hitting the kitchen table? Paul shivered, the coolness breaking his concentration and bringing him back to where he was. Sitting on the stairs, eavesdropping. Not something he wanted anyone to find him doing. He stood up.

'They get me, what makes you think I won't implicate you? Right? Think about *that* before you come on like some nightclub bouncer . . .'

Silence again.

'Stupid shit!'

Mumbling, footsteps, things being moved. Kitchen noises. Then the door opened, light spilled out like a dam had broken and in the glare Paul saw Orlando's shadow. Before he could react there was a click and the light went out. In the pitch-black, his eyes momentarily confused, Paul wheeled round and hurried back towards his room.

He got to the door, turned the handle, pushed the door and slipped inside, closing it behind him. Great, except, unlike before, the bloody thing decided to squeak. As he stood in the room he could hear Orlando coming up the stairs and wondered if he'd heard the noise. He stayed stock-still, his heart thumping, unable to think what to do next. And now he really did need to go to the bog.

And then it occurred to him. Maybe that was what he should do. It might explain any noises Orlando had heard. He didn't really have much choice, cos if he stood around doing nothing for very much longer he was so going to piss himself. Paul reached out, opened the door and went back out on to the landing, trying to act as if he'd just woken up.

He was halfway to the bathroom, and thinking Orlando

must've already got up to the next floor, when the silence was broken.

'Tommy?'

Paul stopped, yawned fit to crack his face and scratched his head as he looked to see who was talking.

'No . . . Paul . . . whoozat?' he mumbled, hoping, as he saw Orlando standing by the next flight of stairs, that his performance didn't look like too much of an act.

The lights came on and, through scrunched-up eyes, Paul saw Orlando, hand on the switch, head to one side, observing him.

'What're you doing?'

'Bathroom?'

'Oh . . . right . . . OK.' Orlando switched the lights out again. 'See you tomorrow.'

'Yeah, right . . .' Paul turned and shambled into the bathroom, closing and locking the door behind him. He flipped the lid up and sat down, taking a deep breath and letting it out slowly. He'd got away with it. Just.

He wondered what the conversation he'd overheard the arse end of had meant. Who had Orlando been talking to? It had sounded serious, the talk of threats and stuff. It *sounded* like he'd been talking to someone who thought he could tell Orlando what to do. And Orlando had sounded like someone who didn't appreciate being talked to like that . . . he liked to tell people, not get told. Dictator geek.

And then, just before the phone call ended, Orlando had made his own threat, something about how if they, somebody, whoever, got him, he'd snitch on the guy on the other end of the line. Like 'I'm gonna *tell* on you!' What kind of a girly threat was that?

Paul finished, stood up and flushed, wondering, after it

was too late and the water was roaring down the pan, if the noise was going to wake people up. Not much he could do about that now. He yawned again, this time for real, and went back to his room. His and Rob's and Tommy's room. He climbed back into his sleeping bag, cold now, and pulled it tight around him. He'd stick around for a bit. Why not? It looked like it could get quite interesting, and he had nothing better to do . . .

14

Tuesday 1st August, Thames House

Jane Mercer had been in the office since well before 8.oo a.m. She wanted to be the first one there, and also be completely up to speed with all the latest information, including the last of the material that had come over yesterday from Steven Pearce in the Threat Evaluation team. She could tell from his attitude he thought the whole Omega Place thing was a complete waste of time – his time, anyway. She couldn't really blame him. There was hardly anything to go on, plus there was the ridiculous 'As Soon As Possible' deadline.

So, here she was, on the first day of the rest of her life, waiting for the two extra people she and her deputy, Ray Salter, had had seconded to them. Once everyone was there she could brief them. On what, she still wasn't too sure. What she *was* sure of was that they were going to need a lot more evidence before they had any chance of closing these people down. Mercer leafed through the papers one more time, allowing her mind to go into free fall as she scanned the pages and let all the facts and figures blend together in her head.

These people were on a mission, and their mission was . . . what? OK, put simply it appeared to be to (a) alert the public at large to the 'threat' to their privacy posed by the proliferation of CCTV cameras, and (b) to actually *do* something about it by destroying as many of the cameras as they could. Without getting caught. That was pivotal. And, as far as anyone seemed to know, nobody belonging to the organisation *had* ever been caught – as in apprehended. But maybe they'd been caught, somewhere on one of their operations, by one of the cameras they seemed to hate so much.

That was what they should find out.

Mercer got up and prised the plastic cap off a metre-long postal tube leaning against her desk. She twisted out the contents, unrolled a large-scale map of the United Kingdom and was pinning it to the massive cork pinboard which covered almost one wall of the room when Ray Salter arrived. He had a backpack slung over one shoulder and was holding two large cups of coffee in a cardboard carrier in one hand and a grease-stained paper bag in the other, both of which he put on the nearest desk.

'Breakfast, boss.'

'Skinny latte, no sugar?'

'No sugar in the coffee, as requested. Plenty on the doughnuts.'

'I'm a fifty per cent angel.' Mercer walked over to the desk. 'Which is mine?'

'The one with the "x" on it.'

'Thanks.' She picked up her cup, popped off the lid and took a sip. 'You're early.'

'You're earlier.'

'Too much to do, too little time to do it in and too few people to do it with. *Plus ça change* with this place, Ray. We've got budget, but not enough personnel, we've got a brief, but a fat chance of answering it. Typical sound-bite

103

decision making . . .' Mercer put her coffee down, opened the paper bag and took out one of the doughnuts. 'Everything looks great on the bloody internal memo, though.'

'As you say, boss, nothing changes. What's going on the map?'

'Red pushpins, one for each of the locations where we know there's been any Omega Place activity. Now that you're here, we might be able to get them in place before the others arrive, which at least gives the impression we know what we're doing.'

Salter efficiently demolished his doughnut in three bites, without spilling any jam, and then licked his fingers. 'Right . . .'

'Very impressive, Ray.'

'Years of practice, boss.'

'Time so well spent. Now come and give me a hand with the pins.' Mercer, still holding her uneaten doughnut in one hand, picked up a small cardboard box and threw it to her assistant.

Salter caught it. 'I was thinking, on the way in, what we need to do is get hold of –'

'The CCTV footage from all the places they've been to?' Mercer interrupted as she flipped open a folder with her free hand and picked up some sheets of paper that had been stapled together. 'My thoughts exactly. Whoever they are, they appear to be clever enough not to get caught in the act, but they could well be on film checking out their targets beforehand.'

'But, if you didn't know this was an organised campaign, why would you spot them, right?'

Mercer nodded, frowning, as she looked at the document

she was holding. 'We'll start putting pins at locations within the M25, OK?' She leaned back against a desk, crossing her feet. 'Thing is, Ray, we have no idea how many people we're talking about here, how they work or who we're looking for.'

'Stuff like this . . . radical, direct action? It's usually small teams, isn't it . . . you know, cells. Highly mobile, too. I'd bet they work in pairs as well, one lookout, one doer; any more would be too obvious. We're just going to have to trawl though a shedload of grainy tape and see if we can see any of the same faces. And there is going to be *miles* of the bloody stuff.'

'*We* won't be going through it, because you and I have got better things to do with our lives than that.' Mercer grinned. 'Like sticking pins in maps.'

'So who gets the shitty end of the stick?'

'I think the lucky winner of that peachy job should be the last person to arrive this morning.'

'Nice. And, once we've completed this,' Ray jerked a thumb at the map, 'what are we going to do?'

'Go digging.'

'For what?'

'More. We have almost nothing right now. Just one set of prints, belonging to one name, James Hudson Baker, who's alive and kicking and *has* to be somewhere. And not forgetting Omega Place, the name itself. It must be called that for a reason, which we have to try and find out. Two needles in one haystack.'

'Twice as much fun, boss.'

Mercer finally took a bite of her doughnut, jam spilling out and running down her hand.

Salter smiled. 'Like I said, boss, years of practice.'

'Know what worries me most about these people?' Mercer licked her fingers.

'No, what?'

'They've got inside information, Ray. Someone's telling tales out of school, and it's part of our brief to find out who it is.'

'And we could be well and truly screwed if we do, boss?'

'Precisely.'

15

Friday 11th August, Kingsland Road

Paul sat in the café stirring sugar into his mug of tea. Another mug was opposite him on the scarred, wood-effect table top, waiting for Sky, who'd gone for supplies – tobacco, papers and such. In this limbo moment, on his own for once, Paul found himself thinking about where he was and why he was there at all. It had been, what – ten, twelve days? Something like that – since he'd arrived in London and sort of become a part of Omega Place. Whatever that meant.

He remembered what he'd thought it meant, when he'd first read the flyer Terri had dropped in the street back up in Grainger. He'd thought Omega Place would be made up of all these people with ideas they were passionate about, that'd keep them arguing for hours. It would all be to do with common goals and action and changing the status quo. All those things he and Dave used to talk about with anyone who'd listen. They'd been called the Red Two for a bit, until the rank and file got bored with the joke, because that was what they seemed best at, getting bored. They didn't seem remotely interested in changing anything, except their hairstyle or upgrading their mobiles or blagging the latest download.

And the bunch he was with now weren't so very different. There were no discussions, no debates, none of that stuff. Any talking seemed to be done behind closed doors,

Orlando in a huddle with Sky, sometimes with Terri or Izzy, who, unlike Tommy or Rob, looked like they took things remotely seriously. From where he sat, in a pale, distant orbit, still an outsider, Paul could observe. They rarely asked his opinion, which was OK because he didn't yet know what it was.

Looking at these people all he could see were six individuals, not really a team. Kind of organised, but not an organisation. Rob? Rob was just your basic thieving sod, who also got a kick out of destroying things. And it was pretty clear that Omega Place was self-financing mainly through his skills and efforts. Assisted by Tommy, who was one of those techy guys who could fix anything, mobiles were unlocked and cars were kept on the road.

And after nearly two weeks he was no nearer figuring out Izzy.

Isabel Morley. That was her full name, but he'd never heard anyone ever call her Isabel. The best way Paul could think of describing her, if anyone had asked him, was small and angry – she seemed to be permanently hormonal and always looking at you with her steely blue eyes like she suspected you of being up to something. Quite pretty, though, in a tomboyish sort of way, but not fanciable in *any* way. Entirely not. Tommy'd told him that he was the one who'd introduced Izzy to Orlando. He'd first met her in some squat where he'd been staying when he'd arrived from Birmingham. She'd been in what he'd called 'a bad spiral' since after she'd left home – and was still travelling down when he bumped into her some time later.

Tommy didn't say why he'd brought Izzy along or why he put up with her bitching, but all Paul could think was that he must have a soft spot for her. No accounting for taste, right? They were tight, those two, but then they were street partners, and although she seemed to give him as hard a time as she gave everyone else, Paul had never seen how it was when they were working together. He'd wanted to ask how Tommy could hack spending all that time on his own with her, but didn't know what his reaction would be – and also, as long as *he* didn't have to do it, was he really bothered?

Before he had time to answer his own question a figure moved across his line of vision and slid into the chair opposite him.

'Man, you were so into your own thing there, you didn't even see me come in, did you?'

Paul focused on Sky, smiling quizzically back at him. 'I was thinking.'

'I could tell. What about – anything interesting?'

'Not particularly . . .'

Sky moved the glass ashtray nearer to him, took a sip of what by now had to be lukewarm tea and started constructing a roll-up.

'You want anything to eat before we get going?'

'Do you?'

'I could tackle a bacon sandwich and win – ask them to make the bacon real crispy, OK?'

'Your wish is my command.' Paul got up; he didn't mind doing stuff for Sky because, with his gentlemanly drawl, whatever he said always sounded polite. 'D'you want another tea?'

'Yeah, why not.'

In London the rule seemed to be that they travelled by public transport. You couldn't get clamped on a bus or a tube and, since they mostly used stolen Oyster cards, it was free as well. Tonight they were going into town, all three teams, all travelling separately, on the one big job. Paul and Sky were on the tube and en route to the Docklands area.

At today's meeting, right after breakfast, Orlando had been like a different person. Paul didn't quite know what it was, except that he was more . . . connected? That was as close as he could get. And there was an energy about him that Paul hadn't seen before, a mixture of anger and enthusiasm that was incredibly infectious and made him feel really fired up. Orlando had said it was time to make a very public statement, time to take the message to the front line. He smiled to himself when he remembered that bit, like they were at war or something.

Friday night, late, when the West End was crowded with tourists and weekenders, was the best time to do it, Orlando had said. A lot of people to hide behind, a lot of distracting activity so anyone looking at live feeds – or, later, at tapes – wouldn't be able to pick out specific faces. Plus they were all carrying baseball caps, wearing hoodies and had with them the kind of loose neck tubes that bikers used, which could be pulled up over the lower half of your face if necessary.

The idea was to mark the whole of Oxford Street with Omega Place material – stickers and a new edition of the Manifesto – like it was their territory. They were, Orlando had said, going to own the place, and they were going to get noticed, get the message to the media and be heard. And Oxford Street was the place to do it. Probably more cameras per square foot there than anywhere else in the Disunited Kingdom, Orlando had said.

That's what Tommy, Izzy, Rob and Terri were doing. He and

Sky were doing a similar kind of thing outside the offices of various newspapers and were now on their way to their first stop, Canary Wharf. Back at the squat, Orlando was going to be using some drone computers Tommy had hijacked to send emails out as well. An information blitzkrieg was how he'd put it.

Paul looked over at Sky, plugged into the iPod Rob had got for him earlier in the week. He nodded and smiled. Paul nodded back. They'd just changed at Stratford, on to the DLR line, and, looking at the map, they had six more stops to go. This would be the first time he was going to work with Sky on a proper job. He did not want to screw anything up.

The only downside of the mission was that, because the areas where the papers had their offices weren't what you'd call big on entertainment, there weren't many people around to see the effect and pick up the Manifestos. But there would be quite a few cameras. Big business liked to keep an eye on things.

Sky had said they'd do a proper recce first, see what they were up against, CCTV-wise, then do what they could as near as possible to the *Telegraph* and *Independent* offices. After that they'd drop stuff around the area, in the pubs and bars.

Exiting the train, Paul could feel the butterflies in his stomach. This was going to be OK. Nothing like the first time with Rob and Terri, no heart-in-mouth climb up a post or anything.

'You been here before, Sky?'

'Nope, never had a reason to.'

Standing on the escalator, Paul looked up and around at

the station, which made anything on the Metro line back home look almost antique. As they came to the top and walked up the stairs you could see the sky had turned a deep, beautiful velvety blue, fringed on the horizon by the glow from the lights of the city. As they came out, he stopped and turned, staring at the buildings pushing up into the night sky all around them.

'Doesn't look like London at all, man. Looks like New York or something.'

'Too clean for that.' Sky frowned. 'Leastways from what I can recall . . . it's been some time since I took a stroll down Broadway.'

'How long?'

'Thirty years, and then some.'

'You miss it?'

'New York?'

Paul shifted the backpack he was carrying, loaded with stickers and copies of the Manifesto, to the other shoulder. 'Yeah.'

'Not specifically. It was just somewhere I visited.'

'Where did you live, then?'

'Milwaukee.'

'Where's that?'

'It's in the middle. About as far from either coast as you can get. Not far from the Canadian border, though, which was handy when I decided to make the one-way trip.'

'You got family there?'

'Some.'

'They ever come and see you?'

'My mother's dead, and my pa kinda disowned me when I took off.' Sky wound the earphone cord round his iPod and put it in his jacket pocket. 'The man was a World War Two

112

vet, had four Purple Hearts, you know, wounded in action? He just thought I was an unpatriotic coward . . . still does, for all I know.'

'You don't talk?'

'Not since the day I left.'

'You ever gonna go back?'

'Life tends not to work that way. Can't ever go back, Pauly, cos everything changes.' Sky shrugged and looked around. 'Come on, we got work to do.'

They'd done Canary Wharf, as best they could. Paul thought they'd be lucky if the right people got the message, but, if Orlando had done his part of the job, maybe the right people would come out looking for the evidence that they'd been there. For some reason Orlando hadn't explained – and Sky claimed not to know why – the whole process of producing the new stickers and Manifestos had been done with everyone involved wearing surgical gloves. They were even wearing thin cotton gloves for working on the street, which, on a summer night, he had to say, felt weird.

From Canary Wharf they'd made their way up to Farringdon and done the same kind of job around the offices of the *Guardian* and the *Observer*, and they were now down in High Street Kensington. Sky had given him a pocket map of the Underground and made him find out the quickest way to get to their destinations. Paul had felt like he was on a trip with his dad, but could see the point. He needed to know how this city worked.

Friday night in Kensington was a whole different matter to Friday night in the Farringdon Road. Even the tube station exit had an arcade of flash-looking shops. This was the last place they were going to do, one building quite near the tube station where Sky said the *Daily Mail* and the *Evening Standard* had their offices.

Paul stayed close to Sky as they came out on to the street, both now wearing their baseball caps and thin cotton gloves. This was unlike anything he'd seen since he'd arrived in London. This was where the money was, and about as far as you could get from the Kingsland Road.

'You must have to be minted to live in this place, man.' Paul checked out the cars as he followed Sky.

'You won't find many pound shops round this part of town, that's for sure.' Sky stopped at a side street. 'This is it.'

Paul stood beside him and looked at the building opposite. 'Doesn't look like much.'

'Ain't what it looks like, man. It's the opinions that come out of it that count.'

Fifteen, twenty minutes later they'd finished the night's work off by putting Manifestos under the windscreen wipers of all the cars parked in the square behind the newspapers' building. They made their way back up to the main road, taking off their gloves, but leaving the baseball caps on; turning left on to a surprisingly crowded pavement, they began walking back to the tube station to start the journey home.

'What's with all the people, Sky?'

Sky looked at his watch. 'Quarter of midnight, coming up to the last train. All God's chillun wanna get home.'

'How long will it take us?'

'If we get the right connections, we could be back at the house in less than an hour.' Sky unwound the earphones, plugged them in and fired up his iPod again as he walked. 'You figured out the best way to get there yet?'

114

'Yeah.' Paul felt in his pockets for the tube map. 'Wait a sec . . .'

He only stopped for a moment, seconds, but when he looked up Sky was nowhere to be seen in the flow of people all around him. It was like someone had hit the pause button – he couldn't move, didn't know what to do, where to look.

The spell broke.

'SKY!'

Some people looked around at him, but none of them was the man from Milwaukee. Paul started to run, pushing his way through the crowds, towards the tube station, cursing himself for panicking like a lost kid. There was only one place Sky was going and all he had to do was catch him up.

As the homeward bound were funnelled past the shops and into the station concourse, Paul found it harder to thread his way through the crush without really pushing, but he had to find Sky. He went for a gap and shouldered his way forward, half aware that someone was yelling at him for pushing. Paul, though, was only concerned with where Sky was, and he sped up, searching for the tall man with straggly grey hair. Which was why he didn't see the two guys, one in uniform, one not, who came at him from his right, stopped him in his tracks and started to manoeuvre him to the side.

It was one of those 'Does Not Compute' moments when the brain can't make sense of the input it's getting. Paul had one, totally single-minded aim – to find Sky – but he had to go forward, not sideways, to do it. And when he tried to shake off these two strangers who wanted him to stay with them, he couldn't work out why they didn't like it and had forced him to stop. And that hurt. Because your arm doesn't like being bent in ways it isn't designed to go. Paul grimaced, and gave up resisting.

'What the . . . ?' He looked properly at the two men. 'What are you doing? I'm gonna lose my friend, man . . . miss my train!'

'It's not what *we* are doing, sunshine.' The man standing in front of Paul, the one in plain clothes, smiled. For some reason, Paul noticed his teeth needed cleaning. 'It's what we think *you* were doing.'

'Me?'

'Yes, you.'

'What d'you think I was doing, man?'

'Thieving.'

Paul was stunned. Thieving? He frantically looked over the man's shoulder, hoping he'd see Sky coming towards him to sort everything out. Surely he would, the moment he saw Paul was in trouble. There was no reason to abandon him, like Orlando said you had to if things went really bad. Like had happened to Jez. But as the crowds momentarily thinned out and he saw the ticket gates, Sky wasn't there.

The room was small and low-ceilinged and harshly lit. Paul sat at the table and waited. After escorting him off the concourse they'd searched him, taken his wallet, mobile and backpack, and then put him in here – he checked his watch for the umpteenth time . . . sixteen minutes ago. And since then time had slowed to a halt. There was just him and the scattered thoughts in his head. Like why hadn't Sky waited? Had he waited and tried to call his mobile, but gone on when he didn't get an answer? And what were these people going to do to him? *He* hadn't *done* anything!

The door opened and the two men came back in. The

plain-clothes one sat down, put Paul's backpack on the table between them and shoved his wallet and phone across to him. Nobody said anything, and Paul looked from the man sitting across the table to the one standing by the door and back again. So, they'd been through his stuff. What was in there that could get him into trouble? Well, now he came to think of it, a stolen Oyster card for starters . . .

'Looks like we got you before you nicked anything.' The man sat back in his chair. 'Who's a lucky boy?'

'Look, I already told you, I was just trying to get to my mate. I wasn't out nicking anything, I was going home, that's all.'

The man smiled. 'Some mate, never coming back to find you.' He glanced at the uniformed man behind him. 'Wouldn't you say, Bill?'

'I would, Keith.'

Paul shrugged. When you're in a hole, like his dad said, stop digging. Don't say anything.

'Want to tell me why you've got these?' The man reached into the bag and brought out the cotton gloves. 'I am *very* interested why, in an empty bag with just a few bits of paper and stuff, you've got a pair of cotton gloves. Almost as if you didn't want to leave fingerprints somewhere, or something. Wouldn't you say, Bill?'

'I would, Keith.'

'Off on a job, were you, sunshine? With your invisible mate?'

Shit. How could he explain the gloves? And what if this bloke took a closer look at the 'bits of paper' and started asking questions about the flyers and stickers? At least they didn't know they were currently plastered all around a building just down the road. Paul shook his head, hoping his face wasn't giving anything away.

'I told you, I was going home.'

'So you did, but what about the gloves?'

Paul's mind whirled. He had to keep calm, come up with something plausible that would get him off this hook he was on.

'Don't know anything about them . . . didn't know they were there.'

The man pushed the backpack with his finger. 'This not yours, then . . . steal it, did you?'

'No . . . I was . . . I was, like, borrowing it. From a friend.' Paul groaned inwardly. What a *lame* bloody excuse, right up there with 'Sorry, miss, the dog ate my homework' in the Lame Excuses Top Ten.

The man opposite him, Keith, raised his eyebrows in mock surprise and glanced at his colleague, Bill. Such ordinary-looking blokes, with ordinary names, who had the power to crap his life up. Or not. Paul had no idea what these transport police were able to do. He didn't know where to look, felt he must have guilt written all over his face and could think of nothing to say that would make them change their minds about him.

'Borrowed, eh? You expect me to believe that, sunshine?'

'I'm not a bleeding thief, man!' Paul jerked forward, wanting to grab Plain-clothes Keith by his jacket and shake the truth into him. Wanted to, was angry enough to, but had enough sense not to go there. 'I'm not!'

'You take a pop at me, mate, and you really *are* in trouble.'

'I'm not . . . I wasn't . . .' Paul sat back in the chair, feeling the tension cramp its way across his shoulders.

'I know *exactly* what was on your little scumbag mind, sunshine.' Keith nodded, smiling. 'Seen enough of your type sitting in that chair, and dozens like it. Haven't I, Bill?'

'Too many, Keith.'

Keith looked at his watch and stood up, pushing his chair back, the legs squealing on the lino floor. 'Exactly, and I don't want to waste any more of my valuable time than I have to doing it.'

Paul watched him, waiting for what was to come next. Nothing did. The two men just stood there in the room, looking at him kind of expectantly.

'Well, piss off, then.' Keith jerked a thumb at the door.

'Me?'

'No, dipstick, the other bloke we've got in this room for questioning.'

Frowning, Paul stood up, picked up his wallet, mobile and backpack and walked over to the door where Uniformed Bill was standing. Were they really letting him go, or was there going to be a sting in the tail?

'I know you were up to something, sunshine.'

Paul turned round, wondering if this was it.

'I just don't know what it was.' Keith tucked his chair back under the table.

'I was up to nothing, I told you.'

'Yeah, right.' Keith rubbed his heavily stubbled chin. 'Whatever you're doing, don't be stupid enough to ever try it around here again. I know your face now.'

As Paul went past Uniformed Bill he could feel the man's eyes following him, like walking past the bully-boys at school when you first went up and were new and the smallest. Waiting for the taunts and the punches had almost been worse than getting them. But nothing happened now, the man didn't do anything, and the door swung shut behind him.

Standing in the corridor, it took him a few moments to orient himself. Then, walking back the way he'd been brought in, Paul discovered the station staff were closing the place up and he had to be escorted out through the already locked gates. He was left standing on the pavement, wondering what the hell to do next. What he should do was phone Sky and find out what had happened, ask him why he hadn't come back for him. Paul got out his phone and found it had been turned off. Why had they done that?

Out on the deserted pavement, with only a few cars driving by on the streets, Paul felt angry and foolish at the same time. He'd been played for a total sucker. Those two, Keith and Bill, had been jerking him around the whole time, scaring the shit out of him and no doubt having a right laugh behind his back. Maybe they had thought he was up to no good when they first spotted him, after the guy shouted at him for barging past, but they'd got no evidence, nothing on him at all.

Except the gloves.

God, that'd been a bad moment, he really thought he'd had it then, but his nerve and luck had held. Lucky, too, that they'd not really looked at the what they'd thought were bits of paper. If he'd had the wit he should've told them he had rights, but cops were so bloody intimidating and he'd just sat there and let them keep him in that room until the last train had gone.

Which was what it was all about, once they'd realised they had nothing on him. A stupid bloody game . . . can't nick him, so we'll dump on him from a great height, make him

120

miss his train. That was why that Keith bloke had checked his watch, then let him go. He was waiting to get his last laugh. The punchline being that he now had to figure out how to get back to the house by night bus.

Paul looked at his watch: twenty-five to one. He switched his phone back on and found he had three missed calls, all from Sky. He keyed the speed dial. As he waited for the call to be picked up he got his wallet out to check nothing had been taken, just for a laugh, and a paranoid thought crept out like a bad smell. Was it still safe to use the Oyster card? He knew it was stupid, the result of spending too much time around Orlando, but he was hungry, stressed and way too tired to fight it. He had no idea what could happen if he did use it, but, just in case, he took the card out and threw it in a waste bin.

16

Saturday 12th August, Kingsland Road

The door opened while Paul was jiggling his key to make the lock work.

'Look what the bleeding cat dragged home . . .'

Izzy, head slightly down and sneering, did her thing of looking up at Paul through half-hooded eyes. Then she turned and walked away, leaving him standing in the door-way. He took a deep breath and walked in. It was just before four a.m. and it looked like everyone was still up. Waiting for him.

Great.

He'd hoped he'd be able to sneak back in and not have to deal with anything till much later, but, if it had to be now, he supposed it might be better to get it all over and done with. Quite why he felt like everything that had happened was his fault Paul didn't know, but that was exactly how he did feel. And, as he traipsed towards the kitchen, dead on his feet, the look on Orlando's face as he came into view did nothing to dispel the impression.

Orlando – sphinx-like, dark shadows under his eyes – sat at the far end of the kitchen table, leaning back in his chair, arms crossed. There was one other chair, at the end nearest him. Guess who for? Paul thought, as he came into the room. The rest of the house was all there, kind of lining the room. Tommy, with a beer, Rob, Sky, Terri, rolling a smoke, and Izzy, still with a smirk pasted on her pale, sour face. Not quite the Spanish Inquisition, but no way a welcoming committee either.

Orlando sat forward, elbows on the table. 'Well?'

'Well what?' Paul pulled out the chair and sat down heavily, dropping his backpack on the floor.

'Did you do everything Sky told you, Paul?'

'Do we *have* to do this now? I'm knackered, man . . .'

'Yes. We have to do this now. Did you do everything?'

Paul nodded, glancing over at Sky and holding his eyes until the older man looked away. 'I did.' Paul looked back at Orlando, noticing the pattern of black stubble on his chin. 'Came back just like you said, man. Took bloody ages.'

'And . . .'

'And nothing. Here I am.'

'Anyone follow you?'

Paul sighed and shrugged.

'Well, did they?'

'Not as far as I know. I was careful, man.'

'Careful, really? So what happened, Paul . . . why'd they pick you up?'

'They thought I was nicking. That's what plod said, that he thought I was picking pockets or something.'

'Why would he think that?' Orlando cocked his head to one side and slightly raised one eyebrow.

'*I* don't know!'

'What were you doing?'

'It was crowded, I got separated from Sky and I was trying to push through people to find him. That was all, and then these two blokes, these couple of police grabbed me and the next thing I knew I was in this room being questioned.'

123

'Didn't you call out or anything, try and attract Sky's attention? He can't have been far in front.'

'Yeah, I did . . .' Paul stopped mid-sentence, not knowing quite what to say. Not wanting to dump Sky in it.

Sky, clearing his throat, broke the awkward silence. 'I was plugged in, Lando, thought I told you. My iPod . . .'

Rob, who'd been looking like the man responsible for inventing boredom, perked up. 'Was that the *Cheap Trick at Budokan* I ripped for you the other day?'

Sky shook his head. 'The Aerosmith, that album with "Love in an Elevator"?'

'*Pump.*'

'Right, man it's . . .' Sky noticed Orlando, forehead creased by a frown, rocking backwards and forwards slightly and drumming his fingers on the kitchen table, and the awkward silence returned.

'So . . .' Orlando's eyebrow was still raised. 'What did they ask you, these policemen?'

'What I was doing and stuff.'

'And you told them what?'

'Nothing, man. Nothing to tell, I hadn't *done* anything.'

'Did they search you?'

'Yeah.' Paul was a crap liar and he knew it. He'd never been able to blag his way out of trouble, ever, and didn't think this was going to be the time and place where his luck would change. He slumped forward, elbows on the table, chin resting on the palm of his right hand.

Orlando leaned sideways and glanced down at Paul's backpack, lying on the floor next to his chair.

'And what did they find?'

Paul blinked and rubbed his face, aware that Terri, standing behind Orlando, was rolling her eyes as she blew out smoke.

'They found my gloves, and what the plain-clothes bloke thought was some bits of paper, so he mustn't've read the Manifestos or anything. I just told him the backpack wasn't mine, that I'd borrowed it off of a mate.'

'He believed you?'

Paul smiled and sat back in his chair. 'No. Not a chance.'

'But he let you go?'

'They didn't have nothing on me, man, and they knew it, too, but they were just messing with me, you know, because they could? I reckon they were keeping me in that room until the last train was gone. Right sods, the pair of them.'

'And that was it, they didn't ask for your name and address?'

Eyes down, not having to pretend he was almost asleep, Paul yawned and shook his head. Orlando hadn't asked about his wallet, so he didn't have to say anything about the Oyster card.

'I was clean.'

'Not quite, Paul. Not quite.'

'Why, man?'

'You'll be on camera.'

'So?'

'So that's not what *I'd* call clean.' Orlando stood up. 'Izzy?'

Izzy smiled, as far as Paul could recall, for the first time since he'd met her; the expression looked kind of odd and unpractised on her face.

'Yeah?'

'Give Paul a haircut tomorrow, a number one. And, Sky . . .' Orlando motioned upwards with his thumb. 'Just a quick word, the two of us?'

Sky nodded. 'OK, Lando.'

*   *   *

'What's the betting we're going to have to move, again, eh?'

Paul turned round too fast in his sleeping bag and almost tipped the camp bed over. 'Move?'

Rob, sitting cross-legged on his bed in a very off-white Adidas T-shirt and tartan boxers, snorted at the sight of Paul's near accident.

'On my life, that'll be what they're talking about. Moving to a new squat. I'll bet.'

'I thought it would be about having a go at me . . . cos I, like, screwed up.'

'Sky should've kept an eye out, man.' Tommy reached down and switched off the desk lamp on the floor between his bed and Paul's, the room's only form of illumination, plunging it into an orange darkness as street light leaked through the threadbare curtains. 'All your fault, really, Rob.'

'Mine?'

'Nicking that bloody iPod and giving it to Sky in the first place!'

'I never told him to turn it up so loud he can't hear nothing else, did I?'

Paul lay staring at the ceiling, now wired and wide awake when all he wanted to do was go to sleep. The previous few hours were replaying in his head like a jump-cut video . . . the moment he was grabbed by the Keith-and-Bill double act; pissing himself in that room, wondering what was going to happen to him; the stupidly complicated route he'd had to take to get back to the house because he knew Orlando would freak that he might have been followed if he didn't. God, what a bloody day. He sighed and turned over, carefully.

'I do not want Izzy to give me a haircut, man.'

'Why not? You'll look a cool bastard like me!' Tommy rubbed his own buzz-cut scalp.

'I'll not, she'll find a way of making me look crap, I know she will. I could see it in the way she smiled.'

'Orlando's rules, Pauly . . . Pisses me off, sometimes, the way he acts like he's some big wheel and can order us all around.'

Paul looked over at Rob, still sitting on his bed in the dark. 'Thought you said he was the boss and what he said went?'

'Yeah, well . . .'

'He is the boss . . .' Tommy belched loudly. 'Ahhh . . . better out than in . . . and nobody makes anybody stay here, do they, Rob?'

'S'pose not . . .'

Silence. Tick-tock. Breathing. The sound of a finished conversation.

'. . . but he *is* paranoid, Tommy, right?'

'Doesn't want to get caught, does he, Robby-boy? It's not like what we're doing is, you know, *legal*. And it ain't such a bad idea about the haircut.' Tommy belched again. 'All gas and no go, that lager.'

Rob sniggered. 'Going out and doing all that stuff wasn't such a good idea, if he wants to us to be low-key. Stay off the radar.'

'Does *he* have a boss?' Paul yawned, tired, but with eyes that still refused to close. 'You know, Orlando?'

'A boss?' Tommy shifted in his bed and the lamp turned on again, this time pointed straight at Paul. 'Why'd you ask?'

Paul squinted, shielding his eyes. 'No reason . . . I just wondered if there was, y'know, someone behind Omega Place.' He shrugged, surprised by Tommy's reaction. 'Like, are there other people out there doing this too, or is this it, the seven of us?'

'No idea.' Tommy switched the light off again.

'Yeah, you do.' Rob sounded like he was smiling. 'You just don't ask questions, just like the rest of us, cos *Or-lan-do* likes it that way. I reckon this isn't all his idea, Omega Place. He's got a real jones about the cameras, but there's someone else, cos the money for the computers and printers and stuff had to come from *somewhere*, and *he* ain't got it, for sure. Reckon so.'

'The cameras are bad news, there's too many of the bastards and who knows what they're looking at and who's doing the looking, right?' Tommy sounded like he was repeating someone else's words. 'You can get spotted by three hundred cameras *a day* in this country – *three hundred*! And it's not made a blind bit of difference to the crime rates neither. Not a bit.'

'Stop trying to sound like you *really* give a damn, Tommy.' Rob stood up, stretched. 'Cos I don't think so . . .'

'Yeah?'

'Yeah . . .' Rob went over to the door

'Where you going?'

'Bog.'

The room was silent for a few seconds after Rob went out, Paul lying on his camp bed that was more like being in a shallow bath, thinking he should probably have kept his trap shut.

Tommy shifted in his bed. 'I do give a damn.'

'Yeah . . .'

'I do. Have you read what he says in them Manifestos?'

'Uh-huh. Picked one up when I first saw Terri and Rob in Newcastle.'

'Then you know. He makes sense, Orlando. Knows what he's talking about.' Tommy turned over and leaned on his elbow, looking at Paul. 'You've seen enough since you've been with us . . . we *are* being watched all the bloody time and *someone's* got to make a stand, right?'

The door to the bedroom opened and Rob came back in.

'You sound like some crap cowboy movie.' Rob mimicked a really bad American accent as he crossed to his bed. 'We gotta make a stand, guys, cuz the cavalry ain't a-comin!'

'Don't you believe in *any*thing?' Tommy sat up. 'This is all just about nicking stuff for you, isn't it?'

'I do my bit, Tommo . . . I'm out there.' No smile in Rob's voice now, Paul thought. 'And you got *no* idea what I believe, sunshine. Not like you and your stupid cross, altar boy.'

'You taking the piss?'

'What if I am?'

Tommy swung his legs out on to the floor and stood up, but he'd hardly got to his feet when Rob's fist shot out and grabbed his T-shirt, pulling him forward almost into his face.

'What if I sodding am, eh?'

Paul slowly manoeuvred himself out of his sleeping bag. 'Hold it . . . hold it.'

Rob motioned with his free hand. 'Keep out of this, Pauly. Nothing to do with you.'

'But . . .'

'I can look after myself.' Tommy's right hand blurred upwards and hit Rob's arm, at the same time as he punched him away with his left.

It all happened so fast in the filtered orange gloom that Paul couldn't see exactly what happened. But he heard Rob's winded grunt and he heard Tommy's T-shirt rip. Before anything else could happen he bent down and turned on the light.

'Cut it out, man . . . no point in this!' Paul said, standing back up to see Rob hunched over, trying to catch his breath and Tommy staring down at his ripped T-shirt. 'It's late, we're all knackered and –'

'My cross . . . where . . . where the *fuck* is it?'

Out of the corner of his eye Paul saw something glint on the scuzzy carpet. He knelt down and picked it up. 'The chain must've broke, man.' Paul glanced up at Tommy as he handed him the small heap of gold chain, and the cross that was still attached to it, and then looked over at Rob, waiting to see it would all kick off again. 'It was an accident, right?'

Rob took a deep breath. 'Din't mean to break nothing . . .'

Tommy stood looking at the palm of his hand. 'Me ma give me this.'

'Right. Din't mean nothing, man . . . I was just talking shit.' Rob's idea of an apology. Paul watched him literally back off, no bravado now, belatedly aware that he must've overstepped the mark in some way. 'I'll buy you a new chain tomorrow, man.'

'I don't want nothing nicked.'

'I'll buy it, straight up.'

'And don't diss me like that again.'

'Yeah, OK . . .'

Paul watched Rob and Tommy, waiting to see if there was any fire left in their fight, whether it would burst into flames again, but it looked like nothing was going to happen. Rob had backed down and Tommy had accepted a stand-off. It was over, for now.

He got back into his sleeping bag and lay down. No more

questions from now on, although he had plenty of them. He turned on his side, trying to get comfortable, the memory of his own bed surfacing in his head, reminding him of what he'd left behind and the strange truth that he'd not really thought about home, or his mum, at all. And then he fell asleep like he'd been hit with a brick.

17

Sunday 13th August, Thames House

The last place Jane Mercer wanted to be, before 9.00 a.m. on a Sunday morning, was the office, but after two interminably long weeks of the whole team banging their collective heads on various brick walls – and frankly getting nowhere – a breakthrough was more than worth coming in for. She opened the office door with her elbow, hands full of a Thermos of coffee and other stuff she'd brought from home, to find that Ray Salter had beaten her in.

'Where were you when you got the call, Ray, round the corner?'

'Was at a friend's the other side of the river, boss.'

'Heard from John and Tony at all?'

'On their way, boss.'

'Has all the footage arrived yet?'

Salter nodded. 'Oxford Street's here.'

'What about High Street Ken, is it on its way?'

'High Street Ken? Don't know anything about that . . .'

'It may be the break we've been looking for.' Mercer went over to her desk to unload what she'd brought in and saw the neat pile of bright green flyers which had been put there. 'I see they've changed colour for Manifesto 4.' She put her bag and the Thermos down. 'Any change of content?'

'Pretty much the same as the other one, lots of capital letters and stuff in bold, lots of banging on about increasing surveillance, the growth of the fascist state, the money it's all costing.' Salter shrugged. 'Nothing we haven't heard before. It's the comment at the end where it gets interesting.'

Mercer picked up one of the folded sheets of paper and turned it over. 'Last para?'

'Yeah.'

'Not more stuff about the remotely piloted flights, is it?'

'No. It's the bit under the "We are Omega Place" heading.'

'Got it . . .' Mercer perched on the edge of her desk, eyes scanning the words on the page. '"*We are Omega Place . . .*"' she read out loud. '"*But who is really running the multi-million CCTV programme in this country? Who looks at all the pictures taken by all those cameras? Who stores them all, and for how long?*" Who indeed?' Mercer glanced at Salter, then continued. '"*And here are the big questions . . . who is making all the money from installing, running and upgrading all this technology? Do you know? Who decides where to put cameras, and why? Do you know? We know someone is pulling strings out there. And we know who it is. Names will be named in Manifesto 5.*"'

'Told you it was interesting.' Salter pointed at the piece of paper Mercer was holding. 'Got a real sting in the tail, right?'

'And makes you wonder where they're getting all their information from.' Mercer stood up, went round her desk and switched on her computer. 'If they were right about the RPAs – which, unbelievably, they were – then it's a safe assumption that there is at least a possibility there's something in this latest assertion.'

Salter was about to reply when he was interrupted by a phone ringing. Mercer picked up her handset.

'Yes? OK, fine, I'll get it picked up.' She listened for another second or two, then put the phone back down. 'We've got a delivery, which needs signing for. Probably the rest of the vids. Can you go down and get them, Ray?'

'Sure. Can't wait to numb my brain with yet more of the world's worst quality surveillance video.' As he opened the door to leave, Salter found himself face to face with Perry and Castleton, the rest of the team. 'Ah, at last, the cavalry!'

Perry stood to one side to let Salter out. 'You going for doughnuts?'

'Unfortunately, no. Video tape.'

'Oh, joy . . .'

The lights were turned down in the Viewing Suite and it was cool, the hum of air conditioning just audible in the background. Jane Mercer came in to find everyone waiting for her.

'Did you bring them up to speed, Ray?'

'Thought you'd want to do that, boss.'

Mercer nodded and pulled out a chair from one of the video consoles. Sitting down, she opened the file she was carrying.

'OK, this is everything we've got, until we go through those tapes. As far as we can tell the "incident" kicked off late Friday night, with stickering and leafleting in and around Canary Wharf, Farringdon Road and High Street Ken – specifically in the vicinity of the newspaper HQs. Then there was the more direct stuff along Oxford Street, real guerrilla action, with cameras being paintballed and otherwise tampered with.' Mercer turned over a couple of pages in the file. 'And, finally, there were the emails, just in case the papers had somehow missed that something was going on.'

Castleton shifted in his seat. 'Why the sudden change in tactics?'

'For some reason they want to get their message to a wider audience.' Mercer shrugged. 'But why now, I have no idea.'

'And what's the High Street Ken footage, boss?' Salter asked. 'Why's that so important?'

'After this whole thing broke a report came in from the transport police.' Mercer referred to her file again. 'Two officers on the late shift at High Street Ken on Friday night lifted a boy they thought had been pickpocketing, but had to let him go because of lack of evidence.'

'And?' Perry made a questioning face.

'And when they searched him all he had in his backpack was a pair of thin, white cotton gloves. Plus, there were some bright green flyers and a few stickers. At the time they didn't mean anything to them, but when they heard what had gone down outside the newspaper offices, they realised that this kid probably had something to do with it. He'd got some story about being out with a mate, and he was acting very suss, but there was no reason to keep him. They did, though, run his Oyster card, and guess which stations he'd been to?'

'Farringdon and Canary Wharf, by any chance, boss?' asked Salter.

'Spot on, Ray. And I think we should have him, and anyone he was with, on the station footage. So let's take a look, shall we?'

18

Monday 14th August, Thames House

No one had gone home on Sunday night. Everybody had taken turns to sleep for a bit, catnapping, really, and had kept going with a combination of black coffee and Pro-Plus. Consequently Ray Salter's eyes were red, his mouth felt like it'd been lined with fuzzy felt and the muscles in his neck hurt like shit. The end result of a night spent looking at hours of videotape. Frame by bloody frame. He stared at himself in the mirror above the sink in the toilet: a face not so much pale as grey, like processed meat, stared back at him. Oh, the glamour, he thought, checking his watch and seeing it was six thirty-ish; probably half an hour or so before any of the local cafés would be open for a restorative bacon sandwich. He was soaking his face with cold running water when the door opened and John Perry poked his head in.

'Ray, you should come and take a look.'

Jane Mercer leaned across the desk and tapped the button that stopped the tape running, freezing the picture on the screen. Then she cranked the tape back a few frames and kept it on hold. The grainy black and white image sort of shivered, making Salter blink involuntarily a few times to try to make it clearer.

'What's this?'

'The kid that got stopped at High Street Ken, Ray.' Mercer nodded at the screen. 'Just before he got picked up.'

Salter examined the high-angle shot. The boy, he didn't look much more than seventeen, eighteen years old, appeared to be stretching up as he pushed through the crowds, trying to search ahead over people's shoulders.

'He's looking for someone.'

'That's what we thought.' Mercer leaned forward, pulled up the exterior shot on a second screen, ran the footage backwards for a few seconds and then let it play. 'Take a look at this.'

The new film sequence showed the pavement outside the tube station; the time and date code said it was 23:47:15 – 11/08/06; the eventful Friday night that had so successfully screwed up the team's weekend. In the crowds milling towards the entrance Salter spotted the kid, straggly black hair, a backpack slung over one shoulder. He was talking to someone, an older man, and then, in the random choreography of street life, as the boy stopped for a moment to get something out of his backpack, a surge of people filled in the space between him and his older companion, who, as he carried on walking out of shot, appeared to be putting a pair of phones in his ears. Neither noticed what had happened, and, when the kid looked up, you could see a look of puzzled consternation track across his face.

Mercer paused the tape and stood up, stretching and massaging her neck. 'He got separated from his friend, then, before he could find him, was picked up by the transport guys because they spotted him pushing his way past people and thought he was steaming the crowd.'

Salter's eyes dodged between the frozen images on the

137

two screens in front of him. 'We know who he is, by any chance?'

'No.' John Perry opened up a notepad and flicked over a couple of pages. 'But we know where he'd been.'

'I love Oyster cards.' Salter smiled. 'They save the general public money, and us time.'

Perry nodded again. 'We don't have his name because it turns out it was a *stolen* card; we do, though, have a list of the stations he went through on Friday night, and, unless you really believe in super-coincidences, matey-boy and the older type were definitely the ones doing the stickering and everything.'

'We don't know where he went afterwards?'

'Unfortunately not, Ray.' Mercer popped a Tic Tac. 'However he got back to home base, wherever that is, the little shit didn't use the card again.'

Salter raised his eyebrows. 'Young, but not so stupid. Must've chucked the thing away when they let him out. Still, I suppose having two faces is better than nothing. It's unlikely to work for the boy, boss, but d'you think we should run the other bloke's mug through the system and see if he crops up? You never know, right?'

'Good thought, Ray.' Mercer nodded, turning to the other two team members. 'We've still got at *least* a couple more hours of vids to trawl through, guys, so don't let me stop you . . .'

The door opened and Jane Mercer looked up from reading through the field reports that had come in about Friday night's Omega Place activity in the West End. 'Ray?'

Salter looked at his watch. 'Everything's been gone through, boss. We can carry on looking, but I think the Law of Diminishing Returns has kicked in . . . I know it's taking me three times longer than normal to do anything and I'm not really paying attention to what I'm looking at, like I should.'

Mercer glanced at the clock on her computer screen; it was almost two in the afternoon. 'OK . . . but tell them to be back here tomorrow, early.'

'You staying much longer?'

'At least as long as it takes me to finish writing a report for Markham so he can send something to the Home Secretary.'

'The story so far?'

Mercer nodded.

'Need any help? As long as it doesn't entail looking at video tape then I'm good to go for a bit longer.'

'Thanks, it'd be useful to just run through what we've got one more time before I commit thoughts to paper.'

Salter picked up a phone and dialled an internal number. 'Let me tell the boys they can piss off . . . John? OK, look, file and store everything and be back here at sparrow fart, all right?' He nodded. 'Yeah, see you tomorrow.' Putting the phone down, Salter pulled over a chair and sat down. 'Fire away.'

Picking up her notebook, Mercer leaned back in her chair and chewed the end of her ballpoint as she scanned the notes she'd written. She glanced up at Salter.

'You got any ideas as to why there's been this sudden change in tactics?'

'What change, boss?'

'I've been through everything Threat Evaluation gave me when I took this gig over and I can't find any evidence they've ever done anything like this before Friday night.'

'Them moving things up a gear?'

'Could be . . . but going from undercover tactics that were more of an irritation than anything else to headline-grabbing activity, kind of overnight. It's a big shift.'

'I reread the latest Manifesto.'

'And?'

'And I think this whole thing was to communicate the threat.'

'Threat? Oh, yeah,' Mercer nodded. 'You mean the stuff about revealing who's "pulling strings". Naming names, right?'

'Yeah.' Salter stood up and slouched around the room. 'Someone somewhere on the inside's obviously been feeding them information, and maybe they've stopped. Friday night could've been a very public warning, you know, "carry on giving us the info, or else"?'

'Tomorrow.' Mercer pointed at her second-in-command.

'What about it?'

'I want you to concentrate on the leak, see if you can get any closer to where it's coming from.'

'OK . . .' Salter stopped pacing. 'You want to know what I think?'

'What?'

'I think it's Home Office, and, if it is, they are not going to give me shit, even if I ask nicely.'

'So don't ask, Ray. Don't ask.'

19

Monday 14th August, Strand, London

The phone went, exactly on time, and Henry Garden grabbed the receiver. 'Nick?'

'Who else?'

'What the hell's going on?'

'You tell me, sunshine. You're more in the know than I am. All *I* know is what I read in the papers and see on TV.'

'But . . .' Garden momentarily took the receiver away from his ear and looked at it, frowning. 'What d'you mean? This is your game, Nick, *you're* supposed to be calling the shots here!'

'Cut the crap and just tell me what you know, Henry. I haven't got time to listen to you whining on. What's happening on your side of the fence? What response has there been to Friday night's extravaganza?'

Garden took a deep breath and made himself calm down, made himself remember that his relationship with Nick Harvey was completely different to his relationships with just about everyone else he knew. But that was because Nick Harvey knew him so much better than most people. Knew so much more about him. Had baled him out of a series of fairly significant gambling debts that could *seriously* have stalled his career, and still could, if the wrong people found out about them. So he owed Nick, in more ways than one, a fact that the bloody man never let him forget.

He was only supposed to be passing on fairly innocuous information that would assist Nick's company, AquiLAN, and its subsidiaries, get rather more than their fair share of local and central government contracts to supply, install and operate CCTV systems. Nothing more, and no great harm done, really. All that happened was that Nick Harvey, a very rich bastard, got richer. And, as long as he did what he was told, Garden understood his debts would remain gone, if not forgotten.

Never forgotten . . .

'So, Henry? Spill the beans, I haven't got all day.'

'OK . . . from what I can gather, they nearly caught one of the Omega Place people, or I think he was at least in custody for a bit.'

'They let him go?'

'Apparently this youth was picked up by the transport police, suspected of pickpocketing, and released because they didn't find any evidence of it. Something like that.' Garden watched the people walking past the phone booth, the flow of humanity, none of whom had the problems he'd got to deal with. He forced his mind back to the business in hand. 'It was only later, after the event, that the officers involved heard what had gone on outside the newspaper offices, remembered the flyers they'd seen the kid had on him and put two and two together. They have him and his collaborator on video tape, though.'

'They do? I need stills, OK? Get me stills.'

'How on earth am I supposed to do that?'

'Your problem, Henry, entirely your problem.'

'What d'you want them for?'

142

'Like you said, this is my game, and I'm calling the shots.' Nick laughed, like he'd made a joke, although Garden had no idea what it might be. 'I want to show them to somebody, so just get the damn things, Henry. Or cats might be let out of bags.'

The phone went dead and Garden was left, the hiss of an open line in his ear, wondering how the hell he was going to finesse this situation. How on earth *was* he supposed to get hold of copies of what had to be classified material? And what exactly did Nick want them for anyway?

Garden put the receiver back down and exited the booth, standing on the pavement, still as a statue, wishing he could stay like that, put his life on hold for a moment while he tried to sort things out in his head. Why he'd ever thought he could get away, unscathed, from the mess he'd made of his private life he didn't know. It was bad enough that he'd run up the gambling debts, acting like some over-paid footballer at the roulette table and playing poker with people way out of his league, but to let himself be put in a position where an upmarket shyster like Nick Harvey basically ran him like an employee was rank stupidity. Except that's exactly what he'd done, and here he was.

Someone almost bumped into him, brushing past without a word of apology, and the spell was broken. Garden looked at his watch and straightened up his slumped shoulders. Back to work.

As he strode along, the very picture, on the outside, of a man in control of his universe, he reran the last thing Nick Harvey had said to him: he wanted to show somebody the pictures of the two people caught by the cameras in High Street Ken. Nick never did anything without a reason, so he must have a plan. And you showed people pictures of other

143

people so that they'd recognise them. Therefore, logic dictated, Nick wanted these two found, presumably so they could be persuaded to stop what they were doing.

Garden stopped walking. *Persuaded.* The word had flashed an image up from his memory banks of one night in one of the casinos he frequented – he couldn't remember which. Not important. What was important was the man who'd been with Nick Harvey that night. He couldn't think of his name, but he could see the man as if he were right there in front of him: average height, but very fit-looking and giving off a kind of don't-mess-with-me aura; wiry, reddish hair, cut quite short; a pale, freckled complexion, piercing blue eyes. He had a way of looking at you, sizing you up, that was extremely disconcerting, like it only took him seconds to get your number. At first glance nothing special to look at, but someone, he'd realised as he'd observed him, who was dangerous.

The man had hardly spoken all evening, playing blackjack in between working one particular roulette table and ending up a good few thousand pounds better off by the time they left. Nick had introduced them – the name still would not come back to him – and had said something like 'If whatever-his-name-was couldn't persuade somebody to do something, no one could', and then he'd laughed, patting the man on his shoulder and said, 'The army's loss is my gain.' That was it, pretty much word for word.

Picking up his pace again, Garden continued on his way, racking his brains for the man's name and as sure as he'd ever been about anything that this was who Nick wanted the pictures for. Whoever was running this Omega Place outfit – and just when the *hell* had it become an *actual*, real thing for heaven's sake? – was going to be in for a shock if

Mr Persuader ever walked in the front door.

And then, with no fanfares, as he turned a corner and came on to the street that would take him back to his office, the name slid out of whatever dark recess it had been hiding in and came back to him.

Dean Mayhew.

Garden smiled to himself. The name to put with the face. Mr Dean Mayhew. The first thing he was going to do when he got back to his desk was find out who he was, where he came from, what part of the army he'd been in. And why he'd left. That would be interesting. Not very hard to get hold of, either. Certainly a lot easier than getting the bloody pictures Nick wanted to give the man.

Garden left the street and crossed the foyer, nodding to the security men who, though they knew exactly who he was, still insisted he take his pass out to show them. Small victories. Everyone, everywhere wants them, he thought as he made his way to his office. Himself included. If he could find a way, no matter how insignificant, to get back at Nick Harvey for lording it over him, he would. You bet he would.

20

Wednesday 16th August, Kingsland Road

Paul caught sight of his reflection in the window of a shop on the high street and for a weird moment didn't recognise himself. Izzy had given him a complete shearing, not a number one, but a sub-zero job, as Rob had put it. He ran his hand over his head, feeling the stubble, which didn't seem to have grown at all since Monday. Probably in a state of shock, he thought, grimacing at himself.

He carried on walking down the street. Now that he'd been about a bit, he realised the area the squat was in wasn't really like anywhere else. Certainly like nowhere he'd ever been before. It was poor and rundown, the kind of place they'd invented pound shops for, but it was alive like street scenes abroad you saw on TV, with all kinds of languages and food, costumes and people. People, it seemed, from everywhere. Tommy called it the Un-united Nations because everyone seemed to just get on with their own lives in their own way, as if they were still at home and weren't in London at all.

And it was an edgy place, with more than its fair share of strung-out junkies and chancers and hoodie-boys, all after whatever they could get, however they could get it. If they saw you had it, they might ask before they grabbed, or simply show you a knife and take it. Even if stuff was nailed down, they'd rip it off. Least, that was what Rob said, but then he didn't really like the Kingsland Road. Way too many foreigners for him.

Skirting round a couple of women who looked like they'd got dressed by wrapping themselves in rolls of vibrantly coloured cloth, Paul glanced at his watch and started to run. Orlando had called a meeting for ten o'clock and he knew better than to be late.

The curtains in the front room were drawn, even though it was well before midday, but that was no surprise. Orlando preferred it that way, liked his privacy. Paul sat next to Rob and Terri on the bottle-green leatherette sofa, picking tiny pieces of the vinyl off the worn fabric of the arm. Tommy perched on the side of an armchair, the one Izzy had commandeered, and Sky lounged, feet stuck out in front of him, in a second not-matching armchair. No Orlando.

Almost as if on cue, both Sky and Terri started to roll cigarettes at the same time, which was when the door opened and Orlando came in, a file and a number of newspapers under one arm. He walked across to the boarded-up fireplace, stepping over Sky's legs and standing, the furniture ranged in front of him in a semi-circle, as if he was in his own amphitheatre.

Paul watched him, aware that there was something about the man that was different today – a difference noticeable, now he came to think about it, since the events of the weekend. Orlando put the file and papers down on the large, sturdy cardboard box they used as a sort of table.

'I think we have made our mark.' He bent down and picked up one of the newspapers, holding it up so everyone could see the page that was turned over and its headline,

147

which shouted *ANTI-CCTV BLITZ!* from the top of the page, above a picture of a camera covered in paint. 'Firstly, well done, everyone.' He looked directly at Paul. 'Even those of us who got a little too close to the action for comfort.'

Paul felt himself go red, his scalp itching, and from the corner of his eye he could see Izzy's condescending smirk coming at him from across the room. Bloody teacher's pet.

'And secondly, I wanted to bring you all up to speed on some changes.'

'So we are moving.' Rob nudged Paul in an I-told-you-so kind of way.

Orlando frowned at the interruption, but ignored it. 'Those of you who've been with me for some time,' another glance at Paul, 'will know that Omega Place was always intended to have the very lowest of profiles, to get our message out at a grass-roots level. This was always the way I favoured, a street-level campaign, because that's where people are, and that's where the invasion is happening.'

Terri leaned forward to stub out her roll-up, head turned so she could roll her eyes at Paul and Rob without Orlando seeing. Paul stifled a grin, knowing she was just taking the mick out of Orlando's over-the-top manner, not Omega Place itself; she believed that what they were doing was a good thing. She'd said so, often enough, and was forever trying to get Rob to take what they did more seriously. But Orlando was making it sound like a religious crusade . . .

'For a small group of committed people,' Orlando nodded at everyone, spreading his hands out, palms up, 'we have achieved a lot, taken the message out across the country at a local level. You have done such a good job that, for all "they" know,' he made inverted commas with his fingers, 'we could be ten times the size or more. But, for all that, I don't think they, the watchers, have been paying attention to us. And I certainly don't think our audience, the public, the people who are *being* watched, have grasped the message either.'

'Sheep,' Izzy said, looking up at Orlando and smiling.

'Exactly!' Orlando reacted as if Izzy had discovered an ancient and long-hidden mystery of the universe. '*Exactly* – sheep, doing what they're told, following their leader, who is a Judas goat, and believing the fairy tales! In the face of *all* the evidence that more and more cameras don't mean less crime, they actually want *even* more of them . . . it's quite staggering.'

'They've lost the will to protest, Lando.' Sky shifted in his chair, crossing and uncrossing his legs. 'Where are all the students on the streets, man? Jeez, back in the day . . .' Sky lit his cigarette again and took a drag, shaking his head as he exhaled, 'youth wouldn't have let The Man get away with this kinda shit. No way.'

Orlando made an exaggerated shrug.

'God, you two sound like a couple of grumpy old men!' Terri sat forward. 'I reckon they've gone out of their way to make politics as boring and crap as possible so 'youth' would get totally apathetic and give up on it. They don't *want* us to vote . . . if less than fifty per cent of the eligible population vote, less than half the population gets to decide what happens, right?'

'But we found them out, didn't we? We know they're a bunch of hypocritical crooks.' Izzy smiled up at Orlando. 'Right, Orlando?'

'True, Izzy,' Orlando smiled down at his adoring disciple, 'but Terri's right, too . . . if fewer people turn out to vote each year, the politicians have fewer people to convince and we get less democracy. The fewer people who care enough to get out and use their vote, the better they like it . . . they want the young to get out of the habit of voting, to believe it's not worth it.'

'Yeah, but me dad says that if voting changed anything, they'd ban it.' Tommy, playing with his cross, hanging from the new chain Rob had bought him the day before, sat watching Orlando and waiting to see what his reaction would be.

'Well, maybe, Tommy . . .' Orlando laced his fingers together and cracked his knuckles, the sound loud in the silence. 'But maybe what they're trying to do, in a *stealth* kind of way, is get the people to ban voting for them by just not doing it?'

Paul waited to see what would happen, wondering when Orlando would get to the bloody point. Tell them what the changes he'd talked about were going to be. His eyes wandered from one person to the next – Sky, looking at Terri; Izzy at Orlando, where else; Tommy . . .

'So, are we moving, or what, man?' Everyone turned to look at Rob, slouched in between Terri and Paul, chewing gum, and he smiled his best innocent smile. 'What? What I say?'

'Yes, Rob,' Orlando sighed, in that way teachers do when faced with a carefully judged, not quite disobedient lack of cooperation. 'Since you ask, we *are* going to be moving on from here, very soon. And we are also going to be ramping up the campaign as well, doing more of what we did at the weekend . . . creating the situation where people *have* to talk about what we're doing and what we're saying. And to that end, while Tommy, Izzy and I find our new base, the other two teams will be on the road, working together. I'm thinking the south-west – Bristol and Cardiff, maybe – as the target areas. OK?'

The back garden of the squat was a tip. It was a wasteland of dying, yellowed vegetation, dead, rusting appliances and weed-covered piles of rubble and broken glass; it reminded Paul of some east European war zone and looked like the kind of place mangy, flea-ridden cats and other even less attractive vermin would probably be calling home. He and Rob and Tommy were sitting outside on a selection of busted-up furniture, sharing cans of lager and snacking on crisps.

'You got the soft option, Tommo . . .' Rob took a long pull from his beer.

'You think?' Rob nodded at him, grinning. 'Well, me, I'd rather be out with you lot, doing stuff, than be a sodding gooseberry round here. Which is how it's gonna happen, right?'

Paul frowned and looked across Rob at Tommy. 'Orlando and Izzy are an *item*?'

Rob and Tommy stared at him for a moment and then launched into a fit of laughter that burst out like a shaken can of Coke. Tommy was the first to recover enough to talk.

'You *blind*, man?' He wiped tears out of his eyes with the heel of his palm as he checked behind him to see if anyone had come out of the house to see what all the noise was about, then lowered his voice. 'She's practically got her head up his arse, she's following him round so close.'

'Terri says she's just about moved into his room . . .' Rob shook his head and giggled as he looked at Paul. '"*Orlando and Izzy are an item?*" Where have you *been*, man?'

'Keep your voice down, Rob.' Tommy glanced over his shoulder again.

'What for?'

'If either of them thinks we're out here taking the piss, I'll get it right in the neck and it's going to be bad enough as it is when you lot go.'

Paul picked up one of the open bags of crisps. 'I just thought she was, like, sucking up?'

Rob, who'd just taken another mouthful from his can, choked and snorted beer out of his nose.

'Give over – I didn't mean . . .'

'We know what you didn't mean, Pauly!' Rob stood up, wiping his nose on his sweatshirt sleeve.

'Yeah, yeah, yeah . . .' Paul sat back, scratching his head, the rickety old kitchen chair creaking ominously. 'What time are we supposed to be leaving?'

Rob finished off his can and heaved it over his shoulder into some weeds, where it joined an assortment of decaying rubbish.

'Tonight, after I've got us another van, big enough for the four of us. Wanna come with me, Pauly? See how it's done, learn a few tricks?'

'Really?'

'Why not? Be good to have someone else can do it in this mob, and not just me.'

'You gonna clear it with Orlando?' Tommy finished his can, squashed it down and lobbed it down into the back end of the garden.

'Sod off, this is my territory, man. And I fancy getting Pauly here up to speed, cos Terri's not interested in learning the game.'

'Your lookout.' Tommy stood up and stretched. 'Who's cooking tonight?'

Paul tipped his head back and finished his beer. 'No one.'

He thought about taking the can back into the house and not heaving it off to join its fellow empties in the urban jungle, but didn't. 'Sky said we were having an Indian, less hassle.'

'Great, a Last Supper,' said Tommy. 'With poppadoms.'

Rob had given Paul the backpack with his tools in to carry. Nothing really incriminating, if they were stopped, he'd said, just a selection of screwdrivers, a couple of hammers, a small Maglite torch and a fully charged cordless Dremel multitool with some of its accessories. It was what was tucked away in a special hidden pocket of Rob's jeans that would cause trouble if it was found – what he called his jemmy, the flexible sliver of stainless steel he used, instead of a key, to get into just about any vehicle he wanted to.

They were going to eat in about an hour or so, about ten o'clock. In fact it was Rob and Paul's job to get the food. Like Rob had said as they'd walked out of the squat, a take-away Indian brought home in a takeaway van.

Walking along the streets, following Rob's lead as he was the professional here and knew exactly what he was looking for, Paul found himself wondering what Dave was up to, back in Gosforth, this Wednesday night. He might be out with a mate, but it was a fair bet that he wouldn't be out with a mate stealing a van.

'You're quiet, Pauly. What's up, man?'

'Nothing . . . just thinking about my friend, back home. Wondering what he's doing.'

'Getting homesick?'

'Homesick?' Paul shook his head. 'No . . . but you miss your mates, don't you.'

'You can always find new mates, man. World's full of

people you haven't met yet, right?'

'Yeah, right . . .'

As they crossed a side road Paul thought about what it must be like to be like Rob, who'd cut all connections with his past and was totally free of duty or commitment. Adrift is how he'd feel, he was sure, but Rob had a kind of total 'no regrets' attitude that meant he didn't ever seem to worry about what was going to happen to him. There was no future for Rob, just now.

Glancing to his right Paul stopped; an N-registration van, the kind of vintage Rob preferred because they were old enough to have little or no security.

'Rob? What about that one, the grey Transit?'

Rob came back and looked. 'Well spotted, man. Let's do a walk past, check the baby out and see if it's worth our time.'

Like a couple of pals on their way somewhere, they strolled down the side street, Rob stopping right by the van to bend down and tie his shoe lace, all the while checking it out. Paul moved nearer the door as he waited and cast an eye over the interior of what looked like a typical working van: dirty, threadbare upholstery, sweet wrappers, junk-food containers and an overflowing ashtray.

'Bit rusty, no oil on the road that I can see, and both tyres on this side are OK,' he said as he got up and started walking again, 'which means, chances are, the others are probably all right as well. I think we should have it away with this one.'

Paul, trying to look like he wasn't, checked the street out. 'Owner likely lives here, right?' He checked his watch in the street light: just after 9.20 p.m. Middle of the week, not a night for going out, no one else about, that he could see.

Shouldn't be any problems. He glanced back over his shoulder at the Transit and felt a nervous flip in his stomach. 'How we, um . . . how we gonna do this?'

'You're gonna follow me and do what I tell you to do, that's how. Simple.'

They carried on walking, Rob making like he was looking at door numbers, and then, as he nudged Paul to cross over the road, Rob started patting his pockets. Muttering to himself about dropping something, he turned and trotted back the way they'd come. Paul, like a dog, followed him.

'Unzip the bag and get ready to give it to me, Pauly.'

Paul swung the backpack off his shoulder as he ran and did as he'd been asked; then he saw a light flash off something in Rob's right hand as they reached the van. Two seconds later, no more, the Transit's door was open.

'The bag.' Rob grabbed it from Paul's hands and dived into the van. 'And get behind the wheel.'

Heart pumping, Paul jumped up into the driver's seat, aware that Rob was down on the floor, the Maglite switched on and in his mouth. He was working on the underside of the steering column.

'Keep a watch on the street, Pauly,' said Rob, voice muffled by the torch in his mouth. 'And be ready to drive as soon as the engine fires, OK?'

Paul nodded, gripping the wheel as he scanned the street. Below him he heard Rob grunting, then a metallic snip and Rob saying something about he'd got it. Paul checked both wing mirrors and in the one on the driver's side he saw a man come out of a house up the street and look back down towards the van. The silence inside the Transit was broken as its starter motor whined into life. Almost.

'Give it some welly, man – don't just sit there, Pauly!'

Paul pressed the accelerator, but nothing happened. And then the starter motor died, making a death rattle, a not-going-nowhere clicking noise. In the wing mirror Paul could see the man was walking their way.

'Rob, time to bail . . . I think we've been spotted.'

Rob shot up from the floor. 'Poxy heap of shit's got a flat battery!' He leapt across the cab and flung open the door. 'Mile a minute time, Pauly!'

Paul exited the van and shot off down the street after Rob, who'd gone like a greyhound out of its trap. Behind him he could hear the man yelling for them to stop. Fat chance, he thought, as the adrenalin kicked in and he picked up his pace, glad he hadn't eaten a massive curry before going out to get a new set of wheels. As he raced after Rob he realised it felt just like the time, years ago, he and Dave had had to pelt away after they'd lit the paper bag full of dog poo outside some cranky old git's house. Ah, the good old days . . .

21

Thursday 17th August, M4 westbound

Terri had been driving for the last hour or so, Rob sitting up front with her. Paul and Sky were in the back of the Renault he and Rob had found and lifted only about twenty minutes after the nonsense with the Transit. They'd stuck in a couple of old mattresses and some cushions and, all things considered, it wasn't such a bad way to travel. Like a band, with no instruments.

The plan was to arrive in Bristol in the early morning, rest up in some car park until midday or so and then do a proper recce of the city. Once they'd worked out the best sites to target, each team would take their pick and prepare their gear. They'd split up around midnight, meeting back at the van no later than two o'clock. To use Rob's favourite word, simple.

Paul sat, leaning against a cushion. Sky was, as usual, spliffed up, plugged into his iPod and listening to some old-school rock he'd got Rob to download for him, and from the front came Rob's choice of music via the CD player he'd jacked into the van's cassette player. Paul took a brown paper bag out of his backpack and fished out the Jamaican spicy lamb pie he'd bought himself before they'd left. It was cold, but tasted hot; the curry flavour fired up his mouth as he ate it, using the bag to catch the crumbs.

On his own, kind of, with nothing else to do, Paul found himself thinking about what Orlando had said, about people believing what they were told. Who were you supposed to believe? If you believed Orlando then everyone in charge was a liar, but then he also thought it was stupid not to vote . . . if you didn't, then you had no right to complain, he said. But, living sort of outside the law, how could anyone in Omega Place vote? He'd wanted to find out what Orlando's answer to that was, but not only would it have probably pissed the man off if he'd asked, but Izzy would no doubt have wanted to rip his tongue out for daring to question him.

Izzy and Orlando. Now there was a surprise, something he would surely have picked up on if he wasn't such a naive bastard. Paul turned and looked over into the cab, Terri and Rob's silhouettes up-lit by the dashboard and the headlights of the traffic coming towards them on the other side of the median strip of the motorway. Was Terri connected to one of the guys and he hadn't noticed that either? Did she have a thing going with Rob? Hardly seemed likely as she treated him like a kid. Tommy? Could be, he supposed, but then he'd actually thought Tommy and Izzy were a pair because they worked together, and how off had that been? What about Sky?

Paul screwed up the empty paper bag and tucked it away behind him, between the mattress and the side of the van. He looked at Sky, a man old enough to be his father, sat, eyes closed and mildly stoned, in the back of this van on its way to Bristol. What was *he* about, still living this weird life, like he'd been in it for ever? What was he doing with someone like Orlando, letting the younger man tell him what to do? Would Terri fancy someone like him?

Sky opened his eyes, suddenly white in the gloom, and stared straight back at Paul, who reddened and felt as if he'd been caught doing something he shouldn't, like he was some peeping Tom.

'Gotcha . . .' Sky smiled.

'I wasn't . . .'

'We've all got this third eye, a real eye right in the middle of our brain, man. Everyone.' Sky sat up, switched off the music and pulled the tiny white phones out of his ears. 'The pineal gland, right? The seat of the soul, some guy called it. It's a psychic thing, like it's how we know when we're being watched?'

Paul smiled. 'Really?'

'This isn't some old hippy shit, man.' Sky tapped his head. 'This is ancient knowledge. The real deal.'

'Were you a hippy, then, before you bunked off?'

Sky's turn to smile. 'My old man would've shaved my head closer than Izzy if I'd tried to grow my hair. No, I wasn't a hippy, I just didn't want to die in some shitty jungle, be the first on my block to come home in a damn box and end up a name on a wall in Washington, commemorating a bad war I didn't believe in. Not my way.'

'But why this?' Paul jerked a thumb at the van.

'Omega Place?'

Paul nodded.

'Because it's what I'm good at . . . being on the outside and messing with the system. I was doing road protests before I met Lando, and this way I've more chance to actually change things, *and* I get to live in houses most of the time, not up some goddam tree or down a tunnel. I was getting too old for all that shit anyway.'

'You believe in what Orlando wants to do, then?'

159

'I believe in direct action, not sitting on your ass and being spoon-fed crap by politicians. And, astonishingly, you guys over here are actually further ahead than almost anyone else in making Orwell's nightmare a reality, so it's a good place to be. If you want to make a difference.'

Paul fell silent, idly twisting the silver ring back and forth, thinking about making a difference and whether, when it got to that time when he should think about going back home and back to college, would he opt to stay, or choose to leave Omega Place? How would either decision affect his future, or anyone else's?

'Sky?'

'Yeah, man?'

'Why's it called Omega Place?' The question had just popped into his head, even though the answer wouldn't help him make up his mind about anything. Maybe now was as good a time as any to ask, because it had been niggling him for ages.

Sky grinned. 'Good question,' he said. But that was all he said.

'Well?'

'It's nothing mysterious, just the name of a place Orlando saw somewhere once, this small street off a big main road, he said.'

'So why pick that name?'

'Orlando said the street was kind of forgotten and probably always would be . . .' Sky stretched. 'The last place that would ever have a camera pointed at it. You know, like a sanctuary. Where they couldn't get you.'

'OK . . . thanks,' Paul nodded as the engine whined and the van began to slow, Terri indicating as she dropped the engine speed down through the gears and crossed the lanes.

160

'Junction twenty, all change for the M5, people!' Terri glanced over her shoulder as she brought the van out of the turn and started to accelerate again. 'Portishead here we come, guys.'

'Terri?' Sky reached up and tapped the back of her seat. 'I thought we were going to Bristol?'

'We are. Portishead's just outside.'

'So why go there?'

'They're one of my favourite bands.'

'Yeah? Who are?'

'Geezer!' Terri snorted, shaking her head.

Sky looked at Paul and shrugged. 'Old fart alert?'

'I've not heard of them either,' Paul said.

'That's what they're called,' Terri said over her shoulder. 'Portishead . . .'

Paul and Sky had their camera sites all worked out so their last one would leave them with just a short walk back to where Rob had left the van earlier in the evening. It was good to be back out and doing something; nervous excitement made Paul feel twitchy and eager to get started, like he was an impulsive puppy and should be kept on a tight leash. After the almost screw-up at the tube station and nearly being caught trying to start the Transit the night before, he wanted to prove to himself that he could cut it. Show Sky that he was OK.

Each of them was carrying lightweight catapults with sights and fold-down wrist braces, plus a pocketful of 10mm diameter ball bearings. In the right conditions they should be able to take out a camera from at least 200 metres away. Sky had recently ordered the cats over the Internet from some company in America who sold them as 'ideal for campers, hunters and backpackers'. And radical street activists, thought Paul as they got to their first target.

It was a twin-camera installation and he and Sky had taken up positions in the shadows, one opposite each unit. Paul watched for Sky's signal – the flick of a lighter – and started counting down from ten as he drew back the thick elastic, feeling the brace pressing down on his arm. He took a deep breath, brought the sights down to centre on his target and let go on the 'one' count. The small silver ball disappeared from between his fingers and almost immediately Paul saw, then heard, the result: the sound of a sharp *crack!* followed by a small cascade of shattering glass. Job done.

Folding the catapult down and tucking it into his jacket pocket, he moved quickly away from the scene of the crime and walked off towards the next place on the list, meeting up, as planned, with Sky at some point on the route.

They knew, as they walked, there was the chance they'd be picked up somewhere by a street camera – there was no way they could take them *all* down. But, with his new haircut, and hood up, in the highly unlikely event someone was actually looking for him in Bristol, Paul reckoned he was hardly recognisable. Even so, the two of them tried, as far as was possible, to keep from being captured for posterity on film as they made their way from target to target. It was just after 1.15 a.m. when they got to the last place on their list, a mobile unit inside a plexiglass hemisphere, the kind of set-up they normally paintballed. They'd never done one of these before with the slingshots and Sky said they should treat it as an experiment – no worries if it didn't work, they'd learn from the experience.

'I want you to shoot as much stuff at the same spot as it takes to bust it open,' Sky checked his pocket to see how

162

many steel balls he had left. 'You got enough ammo?'

Paul held out a cupped palm with ten or so ball bearings in it. 'Should do, shouldn't it?'

'Yeah, OK, that's fine. As soon as the dome breaks I'll go for the camera and then we'll hightail it, right?'

Paul nodded, sighting his first shot midway up the side of the outer shell, breathing calmly and letting go on his own internal count of ten. The steel ball whacked the plastic like a bullet, ricocheting off and hitting an illuminated shop sign fifteen, twenty metres away. A couple of seconds later Paul had fired off another ball, and then another followed that. A large shard of plastic flew away as the third shot hit.

'I got it, Paul . . .'

Paul lowered his catapult, the muscles in his arms now beginning to ache, and watched Sky aim and fire. He saw the effect the ball had as it ploughed into the side of the lens housing, smiling as the whole thing sheared off.

'Nice one,' he said, patting Sky's back.

'Time to go home, man.'

Five minutes later, walking back to where the van was parked, Paul spotted Terri and Rob up ahead. He nudged Sky and quietly began to walk faster up behind them.

''Scuse me,' he said, tapping Rob on the shoulder and making his voice as gruff as he could. 'This is a stop and search . . .'

Terri wheeled around as Rob legged it up the street, almost fifty metres away by the time he heard Paul and Sky's laughter.

'You sods! I could've had a bloody heart attack!' Terri looked up the street at Rob as he walked back. 'And a fat lot of good you were.'

'No good both of us getting nicked, was there? Orlando's rules, right?'

'Coward's law, more like.' Terri turned back to Paul. 'And never, ever do that again.'

'Just a joke, Terri.' Paul put his hands up and made a 'what's with her?' face at Sky.

'Like he said, Terri.' Sky offered her his tobacco pouch. 'Smoke?'

'Yeah, thanks . . .'

'Shift yer arses, man!' Rob snapped his fingers. 'We should get a move on.'

As the group moved on up the street none of them noticed the small, high-res radio-linked camera, positioned unobtrusively on a nearby building, as it zoomed in on them, following them until they went out of sight.

22

Friday 18th August, Thames House

'Ray?'

'Boss? It's . . .' Ray Salter peered at the clock on his bed-side table as he sat up, disoriented, phone pressed to his ear. 'It's three in the morning, boss, what's up?'

'The Duty Officer just belled me. Intel from Bristol . . . they think they've got footage of four of them, plus a number plate. Stuff's coming down the line now.'

Salter got out of bed. 'I'll be there in, I don't know . . . this time of night, half an hour?'

'See you there, Ray.'

'The others?'

'I'm calling them now.'

Salter put the phone back in its cradle and looked at the girlfriend, dead to the world and, lucky sod, destined to stay that way until her alarm went off in four hours' time. He'd leave her a note.

'This operator was really on the case, is all I can say, boss.' Ray Salter was doing what he called shaving by Braille with his electric razor as he walked to the video suite with Mercer. 'He recognised the older guy from the pictures we'd sent out and was keeping tabs on him and the younger bloke – same one as last Friday, just had a serious haircut, far as I can make out.'

'You missed a bit on the left.'

'What?'

'Your chin. You missed a bit on the left.'

'Oh . . . right.'

'What's happening with the plates? Any news on the van?' Mercer held the door to the suite open so Salter could carry on shaving.

'Everyone's looking for it, no sign of it so far.' Salter switched off the razor and blew on the head. 'I've got Perry chasing, and we'll be the first to know, though.'

Tony Castleton, hunched over the desk in the suite doing something technical, waved at them without turning round. 'Two secs and I'll run everything we've been sent . . . they've got some of the new gear down there and a lot of the footage isn't half bad . . .' He punched a button and sat back. 'Take a look . . .'

On the screen a couple of grainy clips ran, one after the other, which featured the straggly haired, older subject the team had last seen outside High Street Ken tube station. Castleton paused the film.

'Our man had just arrived on shift, apparently, so he was all bright-eyed and bushy-tailed when he saw these. They had the pics we'd sent out right near his desk, and he followed instructions just to stick with the subject for as long as possible.' Castleton let the film roll again. 'So then we get the bloke meeting up with his hooded buddy, who I'm pretty sure is the boy he was with last Friday. I got a profile shot off this Bristol stuff and compared it to something similar from the tube station, and I'd say there's not much doubt who it is.'

'Anything else?' Mercer asked

'Yeah, we got lucky . . .' Castleton fast-forwarded the film for a couple of seconds and then let it play. 'New camera, just installed, state-of-the-art.'

The picture wasn't broadcast quality, but it was sharp and it was detailed, the faces of all four people in the frame clearly visible in the close-up shot the operator had got when he zoomed in. A female, blonde hair in a ponytail and wearing a pale-coloured baseball cap with what looked like Japanese characters on the front, and another hooded male, with the original two.

The camera followed them up an empty street as far as the corner where they turned left; the operator, who obviously knew the city's camera layout, managing a fairly seamless segue into a high-quality shot of the group walking off down another street.

'And *then* . . .' Castleton pointed at the screen. 'Watch this.'

The picture remained unchanged for what seemed like ages, although the digital counter said it was only about a minute and a half. Mercer yawned.

'Watch what, Tony?'

Castleton clicked his fingers and a van appeared out of the side road, stopped to check the traffic, then turned right, away from the camera, and drove off.

'So?'

Castleton rewound the picture and stopped it as the van appeared out of the side road. 'Our boy was just sitting organising his thoughts, working out what to do next, when he saw the van and thought he saw something else as well.' He tapped a couple of buttons and zoomed in, stopping as a fairly degraded image of a face filled the screen. The girl with the baseball cap, sitting in the passenger seat of the van, looking down the road towards the camera. Castleton knocked back the rest of his coffee and dropped the paper cup into a nearby bin. 'And that's how we got the number plate. Lucky, or what?'

Mercer sat down behind her desk. She and Salter had left the other two to run the new faces through the system and chase up on the whereabouts of the van.

'Any joy on the leak, Ray?'

'Not a huge amount.' Salter leaned back in his chair, lacing his fingers behind his head. 'I told you that Home Office lot wouldn't give anything up easily.'

'I know you did, but do you have anything?'

'Maybe . . .' Salter nodded and sat forward, elbows on his desk. 'Who would you say knows everything that happens in an office, boss?'

Mercer thought for a second or two. 'Those ex-service types in reception?'

'Correct! You can't hide anything from those types, there's *nothing* they don't see, right?' Salter rubbed his eyes. 'So I did a bit of digging, pulled in some favours and got someone I know to have a quiet chat with the blokes who are in charge over where Garden works . . . decided my best option was to come at this thing from a tangent, see whether there was any gossip, rumour, hearsay or dirt to be picked up.'

'Was there?'

'All of the above, boss.'

'So what did your contact have to say?'

'Not a huge amount about anything we're interested in, but the long and the short is that I'm pretty sure their internal security is on fairly high alert. Something is up, boss.'

'Any particular reason?' Mercer doodled an ornate picture frame on the pad in front of her.

'Nothing specific, just the whisper that whatever it was was inside the building. But my man did tell me that *his* man had said that if he was checking up on anyone, it'd be that bloke mentioned in one of the reports in the file you were given by Markham . . . Garden, Henry Garden.'

'Why him?'

'Change of habits, he said.'

'I don't follow,' Mercer shrugged. 'It's a bit *vague*, isn't it?'

'These guys people-watch *all* day long, boss. It's what they're supposed to do, and noting habits is second nature, part of the game. When someone does something out of character, they notice. And when a person attempts to cover it up by answering questions they've not been asked – like making some crap excuse for going out of the office at an unusual time for them – the uniforms at the front desk wonder why.'

'And that's what put Henry Garden on their radar, leaving the office?'

'Yeah.' Salter nodded.

'Not much to go on, is it?'

'Couple of times he was making phone calls almost the second he was outside the building.'

'Really?'

It was Salter's turn to shrug. 'Better than having nothing to go on at all, boss. It may be clutching at straws, but it might be worth looking into.'

Mercer sketched a stick man holding a telescope. 'Have you started looking into Garden?'

Salter nodded. 'The ball is rolling.'

The other side of the pad, where the stick man with the telescope was looking, Mercer drew a big question mark.

'Be interesting to see if it knocks anything over, won't it?'

23

Friday 18th August, Swindon

A patrol car had spotted the Renault van at around ten in the morning, in the car park of a motorway service area, and immediately called the details in. As the subjects might still be in the vicinity, the uniforms were told to make themselves scarce and find somewhere out of sight where they could keep a watch on the exits until back-up arrived.

Two nearby plain-clothes units descended on the service area, very low-key, no sirens, no lights. As soon as they were able to confirm that the subjects weren't still there, the waiting forensic team went in.

It was obvious from the moment they began working that the Renault had been comprehensively wiped down. Not a useable print anywhere on any surface, which was the kind of thing you expected when up against serious pro criminals, not a bunch of delinquent vandals, like the Scene of Crime men thought they were dealing with. Even the ashtray had been emptied and cleaned out.

So what should have been an easy gig turned into more of a marathon than expected, with everything coming out, including the floor mats and a pair of rather ancient, stained mattresses in the back. Under which they discovered the remains of a couple of marijuana cigarettes and a scrunched-up paper bag that had recently contained – from the aroma and grease stains – some kind of spicy pasty.

Inside the bag, along with some crumbs, there was a till receipt, sodden with cooking oil and its dot matrix print almost illegible. Almost, but, with the tech available back in the lab, not quite.

'Thanks for that . . .' Mercer put down the phone and smiled at Salter.

'Good news, boss?'

'Good and bad . . . they abandoned the van, which had fake plates by the way, at a motorway service area near Swindon; it was wiped down so anything they might have touched was virtually factory clean. Which is the bad news.'

'But?'

'But they didn't quite clean up as perfectly as they thought. Forensics found what they so precisely put as a 'food receptacle' – a discarded paper bag, with a till receipt in it. Dated yesterday. From a shop in the Kingsland Road. The owner of the van's been traced through the vehicle's ID number and he swears he's never been anywhere near the place, let alone went there yesterday.'

'You reckon their home base is near there, then?'

'I wouldn't bet the farm on it, Ray, but I think it's worth putting feet on the street to find out. We've got four of their faces now, *someone's* going to recognise one of them.'

'We got the budget for that kind of activity?'

'We'll find out when I ask, but the impression I get is that the quicker this is cleared up, the happier everyone . . .' Mercer looked upwards, indicating the floors above her, '. . . will be.'

171

24

Friday 18th August, Victoria, London

Henry Garden could not believe his luck. He'd spent the last three days trying to work out how to get his hands on the pictures Nick Harvey wanted from him and had been foiled at every turn. Every time he'd rung in, always on the random numbers Nick had supplied him with and from different call boxes, all he'd had were excuses, which had not gone down well at all. And he'd been so busy with his day-to-day work he hadn't even been able to run the surreptitious check he wanted to do on the Dean Mayhew character, Nick's mysterious 'persuader'.

And then this morning, there it was on his desk, the report to the Home Secretary he'd been copied in on. The one about the latest Omega Place operation in Bristol, which included the number plate details of the van the people had been using. And the possible location of their home base. It wasn't what Nick had asked for, but it was at least something and, on top of that, it was information that couldn't definitely be tracked back to him. It should get him off the hook, at least for a bit, and he'd left the office as soon as he could, making some excuse about an emergency dentist's appointment as he went out of the building.

Garden turned off the main street and made for the phone booth just a few metres away. It was occupied. He stood outside, directly in the line of sight of the person, a middle-aged woman, using the phone, and rather theatrically checked his watch. The woman turned her back on him and carried on talking. For another five minutes. When she finally vacated the booth Garden had to wedge the door open with his foot because of the overpoweringly sickly smell of lily of the valley she'd left behind. He dialled the day's designated number for Nick Harvey, which, unusually, he picked up after just five rings.

'What is it, James? Good news, I very much hope.'

'They hit Bristol last night. Disabled a dozen or more cameras and left their flyers and stickers all over the place –'

'Interesting though that information is, Henry,' Harvey interrupted, 'it's got absolutely nothing to do with the pictures I requested. Have you got them, James?'

'They got caught on film again, four of them this time.'

'How careless of them. *What about my pictures?*'

'They were filmed in their van. I have the licence plate details, and the area where they're probably living.' Garden smiled to himself, picturing the surprise on Nick Harvey's face.

'Why didn't you say so?'

'I just did.'

'Give the details to me.'

Garden almost said 'say please', but thought better of it and simply read out the sequence of letters and numbers and told him about the Kingsland Road location. He was about to tell Nick that the van was a Renault *Trafic* when the line went dead.

Coming out on to the pavement Garden started to cross the road, wrinkling his nose as he tried to work out which was worse, the air quality in the booth or outside it, just as a cyclist came down the street the wrong way. Leaping backwards he cursed the two-wheeled blight of bike couriers, checked the road again, then set off back to the office.

Garden didn't notice that the courier had stopped a little way down the street. Nor did he realise the man was watching him from behind his wraparound dark glasses as he spoke into the walkie-talkie attached to the strap of his shoulder bag.

25

Friday 18th August, Kingsland Road

Paul saw a space coming up on his left and slowed the van down; there was no one behind him, but he indicated anyway, pulling up, selecting reverse and slowly feeding the Toyota into the gap between two cars. Rob had picked this van out from a motorway service area car park near Swindon, insisting they had to change vehicles; Paul couldn't work out if all the swapping was strictly necessary, or if it was just that Rob liked nicking motors. Now its job was done they were abandoning it to its fate on some skanky north London street.

Terri wound her window down and took a look. 'Not bad . . . a crack shot with the catapult, *and* he can park. Your essay on "What I Learnt on my Holidays" is going to make interesting reading.'

Paul shot her a glance as he straightened up. 'Who says I'm going back anywhere that I'd be writing an essay?' He cut the engine. 'Eh?'

'OK, so you're not going back anywhere . . . I thought you probably would be.'

'Why?'

'I dunno . . .' Terri reached down and picked up the plastic carrier bag from the floor by her feet. 'Come on, let's clean up this heap and get back, I'm bloody starving.'

Paul took the rag Terri handed him, but didn't do anything with it. 'Why?'

'Look, I didn't mean anything, OK . . . I just got the impression you were coming down here for some laughs, not for ever.' She took a spray cleaner out of the bag and pumped some on to her bit of cloth. 'Don't you miss anyone up there?'

'Maybe. What about you?' Paul took the spray off her. 'You got nowhere to go back to?'

Terri didn't say anything, not looking at Paul, concentrating all her energies on rubbing the dashboard and glove compartment. 'I feel as if I left home when I was, like, twelve,' she said, still not looking at him. 'Like it's just been me since then.'

'Why's that?'

Terri stopped wiping the dashboard and turned her head, face shaded by the peak of her pale baseball cap. 'Cos that's when they shoved me off to boarding school.'

'*Boarding* school? You don't –'

'I don't what?'

'You don't, like, sound that way . . .'

'What way?'

'Y'know, posh.'

'You repeat one word of this, Paul, and I will –'

'They don't know about it, the school and stuff?'

'My little secret.'

Paul ran the cloth over the steering wheel and then the gear stick and handbrake. 'Reckon they'd take the piss about it?'

Terri wiped the door handle and then opened the door. 'What d'you think? I'd never hear the last of it from Rob.'

'Why tell me, then?' Paul cleaned the driver's side-door

176

handle and got out, locking the door before slamming it shut. He walked down to the back of the van where Terri was waiting.

'Probably shouldn't've done.' Terri nodded at the rear doors. 'Reckon the inside needs going over?'

'Better had.' Paul lifted the handle, pulled open the door and climbed up. 'I won't tell, trust me.'

'Better bloody not.'

Paul looked sideways at Terri as they gave the interior of the van a quick once-over. That was the trouble with girls. You could never tell, when they were nice to you, if it was because they 'just wanted to be friends' or because they 'liked you, but not in that way'. He knew he liked Terri, very much in that way, but didn't dare do or say anything that might let him find out exactly how she felt. He wanted to know, but he wanted hope, not disappointment.

He remembered the words of some rock ballad his dad always sang, if he was a bit pissed – so it happened quite often – and he'd been talking about breaking up with his mum.

'*And then the question seemed to turn out wrong,*' it went, his dad belting the words out in his raspy cigarette voice. Which was just how he felt, that he'd say something stupid and Terri would walk away, like his mum had. History repeating itself.

On the way back to the house Terri's mobile went. She listened, nodding, then cut the call.

'Got to go to the shops.'

'What for?'

'Can we get some stuff for a stir-fry, and the evening paper.'

'Must mean Sky's cooking.'

'Just as long as it's not Rob.' Terri rolled her eyes and gagged. 'Rob doesn't think it's proper food if it's not deep-fried or doesn't come out of a can.'

'Or chocolate. I reckon he'd maybe eat a carrot if it was covered in chocolate.'

'True.' Terri laughed at the thought.

'D'you think we'll be in the papers again?'

'Orlando'll be pissed off if we aren't. Don't know why he's changed his mind about how we do things, why he wants all this publicity suddenly. Doesn't make sense.'

Paul thought back to the conversation he'd overheard Orlando having on the phone, the night he'd arrived in London. It had sounded like he was having an argument with a boss or business partner, but Omega Place wasn't a business and Orlando didn't seem like the kind of person who went in for partners.

He wondered if he should tell Terri what he'd heard. She might know more and be able to figure out what had been going on. On the other hand, she might think he was a total creep for eavesdropping like he had, and then grass him up to Orlando. It wasn't worth the risk. Maybe that conversation had had nothing to do with anything, and probably the fact that he knew about it should stay *his* little secret.

They were out in the back garden again, Paul and Rob and Tommy and some cans. The Three Muskebeers, Tommy had called them. Terri was back inside, helping Sky in the kitchen, and Izzy probably wasn't doing anything like what Rob's fevered imagination was continually dreaming up. Paul had thought about staying in the kitchen as well, but knew he'd end up with some shitty skivvy job if he did.

178

Rob popped his can and took a drink. 'You find us a new place yet, Tommy?'

'Nope . . .' Tommy opened his can. 'I did sod all about it, me.'

'Why, man? I thought the Big Boss Man had spoken, like, and we were on the move?'

'He spent the entire bloody day writing, didn't he? A new Manifesto, he said.'

'What about Izzy, what was she doing?'

'Helping him.'

Rob leered. 'I bet she was!'

'She was. They were down here, man, all day. Getting dead serious about "the next message to the people", he called it.'

'Wonder why he changed his mind?' Paul chose the least rickety chair and sat down.

'He kind of got fired up, this morning, after he got a phone call.' Tommy picked up a piece of rubble and lobbed it down the garden. 'He didn't answer it or anything, just swore at the phone and turned it off. Told me to lose that number and to fix him up a new one. So I spent most of today mucking round with mobiles.'

Paul took a drink from his can. Another phone call. From the same person he'd heard Orlando talking to before? Yeah, right, why think that? Probably his mum. He grinned to him-self, wondering what a radical activist's mum would be like, imagining this female version of Orlando telling him right-on, socialist, propaganda bedtime stories . . .

26

Friday 18th August, Hendon

Dean Mayhew put the phone down. Thank Christ for that. Something to do, at last. He'd been hanging round, twiddling his sodding thumbs, for days, waiting for Nick Harvey to call. He was on wages, good wages, but even so, he hated doing nothing and there were only so many times you could dismantle, clean and put back together various parts of your motorbike. Or your guns. And Dean had quite a lot of guns, for someone who lived in a very average suburban house in north London and whose neighbours thought he was something to do with insurance, which in a way he was. He ensured that the things his clients wanted to happen did happen. And vice versa.

He'd worked, on and off, for Harvey's company, AquiLAN, for quite a few years now. They were good clients. But this was the first time that the boss man had ever been so personally involved in a job, although, he thought as he made himself a cup of filter coffee, there's always a first time for everything. Dean boiled the kettle and poured the water on to the single-cup cafetière, already making a mental 'To Do' list. He'd be leaving the house within the next twenty minutes.

Harvey hadn't given him much to go on. The only real piece of information he'd got was that the people he was after were thought to be holed up in some squat in the

Kingsland Road area. No more and no less than the police had, so Harvey said. Nothing, really. Apart from the fact that he could tell these Omega Place people were a cautious bunch. He liked their style. Seemed professional, not a bunch of chancers, even though they'd screwed up in Bristol and got properly caught on camera in their van. Still, if people didn't make mistakes his job would be so much harder.

His job was to find the Omega Place operation, then close it down. No negotiation. Things had already progressed well beyond that, which was why he'd been called in. He preferred the no bullshit, in-and-out jobs. Black and white work, he thought of it as. No grey areas.

Upstairs he packed his tank bag and a small backpack, chose a fake ID pack from the selection he had available, locked everything either incriminating or valuable up in the floor safe hidden under his bed and went back downstairs. There was nothing in the house that needed looking after while he was away – no plants, no pets and certainly no partner – and once he'd activated the alarm the place was pretty secure. The system he'd had installed was hard-wired to a central control, which sent the law round if it was activated, which, considering what he did, he thought was quite ironic.

It hadn't taken him long to get over to the Kingsland Road area on the Yamaha. The first thing he did was check all the local newsagents for people offering rooms to rent; he was moving in until the job was done, which could mean a couple of days, maybe even a working week, if he was unlucky. Not that Dean believed in luck, way too risky. Instead he relied on an almost obsessive attention to detail and a ruthless efficiency, a combination that had worked well for him so far in his career.

It took him an hour or so, but he finally got what he wanted: a room – first floor, front – in a house with off-street parking for the bike at the side of the house. He rented the place for a month, paid in cash and told the landlord he was a contract computer programmer from out of town, working shifts for an office in the City. He intimated he could be a regular customer.

The bedsit was tacky, basic, but reasonably clean – though it hardly mattered as Dean didn't intend to spend very much time there. As soon as he'd stowed everything he didn't need to carry with him well out of sight, he went out to a nearby hardware shop. Half an hour later he'd replaced the Yale lock on his door, just in case the landlord felt like poking around. Then he went out to start tracking down his prey.

Standing on the street, he gathered his thoughts. He knew next to nothing about this place, but what he did know was that the people who really had an area totally sussed were the postmen. Everyday they walked up and down each street, went past every door. If anyone could tell him where the squats were, the posties could.

His story was simple, almost a cliché, because simple was easy to tell, easy to understand, and much easier to believe than complicated. He was looking for his kid brother, who'd left home a year or so ago and come down to London from a village outside Wolverhampton. Usual thing, looking for excitement, looking for streets paved with gold, same old same old. A good kid, just a bit naive, you know?

The reason he was here was that their mum had fallen ill

and it didn't look good. She was likely going to die, and she knew it . . . wanted to see her boy one last time. Dean hadn't laid it on too thick, just enough to do the job. Which it had.

His sob story had succeeded in getting him in contact with the shift foreman, who had been very sympathetic. Except Dean didn't want sympathy, what he wanted was some addresses of squats in the local area where his 'brother' might be staying. Find the information he needed to get a move on. Get back out on the street.

But sometimes you had to wait. Be polite and listen.

Dean could do that, for a bit, although he had to work really hard at not looking at his watch as the man rabbited on and on about the state of the nation and how unappreciated postmen were. Finally, when he thought he'd given enough of his precious time, he stepped into a gap in the conversation.

'I'm sorry, mate, but, you know, I've, um, I've things to do . . .'

The shift foreman checked the time himself, as if, somehow, they were working to a similar schedule. 'Oh, right . . .'

'Could I have the addresses?' Dean pointed to the folded piece of paper in the man's hand, the result of a straw poll he'd taken in the sorting office.

'Yeah, sure . . .' The foreman handed it over, slightly put out at being interrupted.

'And thanks.' Dean shook his hand, leaving a twenty-pound note in the man's palm, and left.

There were half a dozen addresses on the list, which, looking at the A–Z street map, were spread out either side of the main road. Walking it was the only way to check out each place properly and he had no time to waste. The opposition, whichever bits of the law were also out there looking for these people, was not going to be that far – if at all – behind him. The clock was ticking, and if he wanted to be paid, he had to be first in the race.

He knew the law had pictures of the four people caught on camera in Bristol, but didn't know how good the images would be. He knew they would, like him, be looking for the squat these people were living in, so they would both be playing the game by very similar rules. Except he had one advantage. He had a picture of the man in charge, and they didn't. And the man in charge was the only one he cared about.

Nick Harvey had been at university in Birmingham with him; the way Harvey told it, both had been heavy-duty politicos in the student union. Right-on rabble-rousers, is how he'd described the two of them back then. Harvey'd said that he'd done it to get the girls, and as soon as his student days were over he'd ditched the left-wing crap and joined the dirty capitalists. Money, he'd realised, being a much better way of attracting the kind of women he liked than radical politics. And Dean wouldn't argue with that.

Harvey's friend had gone the other way, though, become even more extreme, but the two of them had, somehow, remained friends and remained in contact over the years. Harvey hadn't explained why, and, frankly, Dean didn't care.

It was just after eleven o'clock when Dean pushed open the door of the Vietnamese restaurant and asked if they were still serving. They were, and over the first food he'd had since early that morning, he listened to the comments he'd made on his tiny digital recorder and looked at the notes and sketches he'd made about each of the houses on his list.

Two were empty and boarded-up, which meant the bailiffs must've been in and regained the property for the owner. Of the others, there was a party going on at one and he'd actually managed to get in and have a poke around, straight as he looked, with his cover story. It wasn't the place he was looking for, unsurprisingly.

And that left him with three houses needing a closer inspection, one of which he had really good feelings about. Something about the way every window at the front was heavily curtained, keeping the gazes of the curious at bay, drew him to it. He'd also checked the next road down. A top-floor flat, which should give him some kind of view of the rear of the target house, was for sale. He'd left a message on the estate agency's answerphone service, saying he was a cash buyer, very interested in the property, and requesting a viewing as soon as possible. He would be there when they opened up tomorrow morning.

Dean wasn't that tired, but he was going to be up with the milkman in the morning, checking the three houses out in daylight and before there was any activity. Finishing his meal, he paid his bill and left the restaurant. As he walked back to the bedsit he saw someone talking to a man running an all-night minimarket, leaning across the counter and showing him what looked like photographs. If this was one of the team looking for the same people he was, they were really going for it.

Dean frowned, frustrated that there was nothing else he could do right now, except wait until the morning. Which might be too late. Then he stopped and went into the shop, picking up a chocolate bar and standing behind the man

185

with what he now saw were photos. He heard him ask the shop owner if he was sure he hadn't seen any of the people, and watched the man shake his head.

'Lost someone?' Dean asked, as the questioner turned to go, putting a concerned look on his face.

The man, shorter than him by an inch or so, nodded and Dean could tell he was tired. 'Yeah.' The man held out four black and white pictures, which Dean took. 'Seen any of these people round here?'

Dean examined each photo carefully, committing the faces of the older man, the two boys and the girl to memory; it was a skill he'd honed to perfection over the years. Then he looked up, giving the pictures back.

'No, mate, sorry.'

27

Friday 18th August, Tunbridge Wells

Henry Garden sat in the armchair in front of the TV. He wasn't paying any attention at all to what was happening on the screen. His mind was elsewhere, trying to deal with what he'd just read. He glanced over at the six-seater table behind him in the lounge-cum-dining room of his flat, at his laptop, open and still displaying the file he'd copied on to a USB flashdrive in the office. Dean Mayhew's army record.

Garden stood up and went into the kitchen to pour himself another large glass of wine. He'd finished the first one without even knowing he was doing it. Coming back out he went over to the table and sat down in front of his computer, scrolling to the top of the document and reading it through again, hoping he might have made a mistake, misunderstood some highly relevant piece of information that would change everything. It was a vain hope. He hadn't.

It was all there in black and white. Dean Mayhew was a dangerous and unstable man. Ex-SAS. Trained to kill, and seemingly very good at his job. His only problem was that he'd apparently found it almost impossible to differentiate between the theatre of war and life away from the combat zone. He was a complete wild card, as far as Garden could make out, and had been 'let go', Services No Longer Required, some five or six years previously. One violent incident too many. When Nick had introduced him to Mayhew, at the casino, he must only have been out for a year or so.

He was, according to his psych profile, a highly intelligent, if badly educated, man with sociopathic tendencies. Was that as bad as being psychopathic? For the life of him Garden couldn't remember, and for one horrible moment he was catapulted back into a classroom at school. The room where his sadistic English teacher, Mr Bailey, had delighted in exposing any and all examples of what he called 'the rampant stupidity of this ghastly excuse for a generation'.

Garden reached behind him for his dictionary, pulling it off the shelf and opening it. This was, he thought, as he flicked through the delicate, petal-thin pages, one of the best reasons for living alone: everything was always exactly where you expected it to be.

Sociopath, he read, *An individual with a personality disorder that manifests itself in extreme antisocial attitudes and behaviour, as well as a lack of conscience.*

Nice. He flicked backwards and stopped at another page.

Psychopath, it said, *A person suffering from a chronic mental disorder, with abnormal or violent behaviour.*

From the Greek *psyche*, the soul, and *pathos*, meaning disease. Disease of the soul . . . it almost sounded tragic when put like that.

Not a lot to choose from there, then. Returning the book to where it belonged, Garden felt the cold aura of panic descend again, the sense that things were beginning to unravel uncontrollably and that it was all his fault. Which it was. Dean Mayhew was not a very nice person, and one to whom Garden had effectively handed the information he needed to find a group of people; people Nick Harvey wanted found and stopped. And the only reason you'd use a man like Mayhew was if you wanted them stopped permanently.

188

Garden was sure he could feel his heart pounding much too fast as he closed the file and shut down the laptop. He wished he could press an 'undo' button, like on his computer, so that he would never have met Nick Harvey, never have heard of AquiLAN. What was the man doing associating with aberrant dross like Mayhew anyway?

There was nothing intrinsically bad, or evil, with the idea of creating an anti-CCTV unit, which had been Nick's original plan behind the idea of Omega Place. But there was *a lot* wrong with hiring a maniac like Mayhew to clear up the mess when your own creation refused to obey orders and started to threaten the status quo.

And even though Garden had known about the project right from the start there'd been nothing he, personally, could have done to put a stop to it. Harvey – a man whom he'd once heard described as having the morals of a horny wolverine – had him, figuratively speaking, hanging by his thumbs, his toes just touching the ground. There was nothing he could have done, not with Nick holding the substantial . . . really *very* substantial gambling IOUs over his head. And whatever other evidence the man now had of his continuing involvement.

The idea had seemed harmless enough, to begin with. Nick would use an old contact of his from university days to set up and run a fake, virtual anti-CCTV radical action group. This person, Garden had never met him, apparently knew all about agitprop and street protests and he would make Omega Place seem like the real thing, as well as an operation that appeared bigger than it actually was. Seem like the real thing, not actually *be* the real thing.

The plan had been for the group to operate in areas where AquiLAN had already got contracts in place, but wanted to expand the business possibilities. Omega Place's anti-social activities, the perceived increase in vandalism and quasi-criminal behaviour – all reported in the local press – would give the impetus needed to persuade the public that more cameras were necessary. And councils that it was money well spent. A win-win situation all round.

Where had it all gone so wrong?

Garden knew he was kidding himself by asking the question. He knew precisely when it had all gone pear-shaped. When he'd had one of his good nights at the tables and had had too much to drink; he'd told Nick about the remotely piloted vehicle programme, and the next thing he knew the idiot had told the person running his covert operation and *he'd* put the information in print. The highly *classified* information.

As if that wasn't bad enough, it seemed like Nick's plan had backfired and his pet project wasn't as under his control as he'd thought. From what Garden could work out, the man in charge had had another agenda and pulled a fast one by getting Nick to fund setting up Omega Place, then running off with it. The tail had started to wag the dog.

Never trust a radical . . .

28

Saturday 19th August, Kingsland Road

The sign in the window had stated, quite clearly, that the estate agency opened at 9.30 a.m. The first employee to make it in swanned up to the front door at about 9.52 a.m. Dean, a stickler for timekeeping, only just managed to keep his temper under control, his left hand holding his clenched right fist tightly behind his back so that he didn't throttle the stupid little nancy boy or punch his lights right out.

As luck would have it, the flat had turned out to be a vacant possession and the agent had turned out to be an idle little sod, quite willing to hand over a set of keys, so Dean could show himself around. So here he was, in the small second bedroom, which gave him the best view on to the rear of his target house, with a cup of reasonable take-away coffee, a bacon and egg sandwich and a newspaper. And his digital camera. It was now set up on its tripod and pointing out of the open window, zoomed in on one of the back bedrooms – as good as a pair of binoculars. So far, nothing. No sign of any movement in any of the rooms. Maybe they'd had a late night.

Dean finished his breakfast, putting the paper bag the sandwich had come in inside the empty paper cup and dropping that into the small carrier bag he'd been given in the café. He checked his watch. 10.55. If someone didn't get

191

up soon he'd have to go round and knock on the bloody front door. He checked the LCD screen on the camera, switching to viewfinder mode, and then shifting the camera so it was looking at what he assumed might be the kitchen. He adjusted the zoom. Was that a movement, or just a reflection on the window pane? He fine-tuned the camera angle and concentrated on the image, hardly breathing, like he would if he was staring down the scope of a sniper rifle. Waiting for the shot.

It was movement. No doubt about it.

Lightly touching the shutter release to lock the focus on the back door, Dean left his finger hovering over the button. Waiting. Now something was happening and he was switched to active mode; now he didn't mind the waiting because there was a purpose to it. He would soon know if he'd been right and this was the house he wanted. He was sure this was the place, trusted the instincts that had served him well all his professional life – when he didn't let his bastard side ride roughshod over them.

The handle on the back door moved slightly . . . moved some more and then, finally, the door opened. A girl came out and Dean had framed her, checked the focus and fired off a couple of shots before he realised she didn't match any of the pictures he'd been shown the night before. Dark, shoulder-length hair, oval face, slim. His view of her from this bedroom was at a similar angle to the shots taken from the CCTV footage that he'd seen, and she was definitely not the girl. That one'd been fair-haired. He took a pad out of his jacket pocket and checked the notes he'd written after getting back to the bedsit. Definitely fair-haired.

Had he got the wrong place? Always a possibility, because he really hadn't a whole lot to go on with this situation.

Dean closed out the negative thoughts and looked through the viewfinder at the open door. Was there someone else in there? Would they come outside as well? Back to the waiting game. He watched as the dark-haired girl went inside again. And waited some more, standing still as a cat about to pounce, feeling like a coiled spring. Powerful, but in control.

Someone, someone male, walked into shot . . . *CLICK-CLICK-CLICK* . . . and then out of shot. Followed almost immediately by someone else, also male, before he had time to look properly at who he'd just photographed . . . *CLICK-CLICK-CLICK*.

Quickly switching to viewing mode, Dean scanned the shots of the two people, two young men. Both very similar in build, age and appearance, both with close-cropped hair, both very like one of the pictures the man had shown him in the minimarket, although one had a squarer jaw than he remembered. Reselecting the shooting mode, Dean zoomed back out and panned the camera until he'd found the pair, one of whom now had his back to him. Either of them *could* be who he wanted. But, to be sure this really was the right place, he needed to see another person, another possibly-maybe. Two maybes and he had somewhere worth properly checking out.

A couple of minutes later somebody else came out of the house. And this time there was no 'maybe' about it. This was definitely the older guy with the straggly hair and moustache, dressed pretty much as he had been in the picture; no need to check his notes this time. Bingo. The waiting was over and he could move forward to the next stage as this had to be the bolt hole where Orlando Welles was hiding.

Dean took a couple of pictures of the man as he talked to the two boys, shut the camera down and took it off the tripod. Putting everything away in his backpack, he picked up the carrier bag with his rubbish and checked he'd left nothing at all behind. He went over and closed the window and then left the flat.

29

Saturday 19th August, Kingsland Road

Everyone had slept in late, for some reason. And here it was, just after eleven o'clock and Sky had just come out to ask him and Tommy what they wanted for the brunch he was offering to make.

Tommy looked surprised. 'Is there enough food in the house, man?'

'There will be when you two guys go and get some in.'

Paul laughed, noticing the flash of light as the sun caught an upstairs window someone in a nearby house was closing. 'Always a snag, isn't there?'

'No such thing as a free breakfast, right?'

'Is there enough cash?' Tommy yawned. 'Or are we gonna have to use one of Rob's dodgy credit cards?'

Sky dug into his jeans pocket and pulled out a twenty-pound note. 'I think I've got enough. A Jackson should do it.'

Tommy reached for the money. 'If it wasn't so late I'd get us all breakfast from McDonald's for that much!'

Sky moved the note out of Tommy's reach. 'And I'd be pretty pissed if you did. I want eggs, free range, I want bacon, sausage – the thin kind – and I want OJ, that Greek bread with the sesame seeds on top, not the white sliced shit, and some tomatoes. We have butter and we have milk and we have coffee.' He gave the money to Paul. 'Go . . .'

*　　*　　*

For all Sky's attempts to raise the spirits in the house, nothing seemed to work. Orlando was in a foul mood because he'd lost a file on his computer and was going to have to write the new Manifesto from scratch again, and Izzy somehow felt that it was her duty to be monosyllabic and grumpy in sympathy. For whatever reason, Rob and Terri weren't talking either, and by the time he'd finished helping Tommy with clearing up the debris, Paul wanted out. It was too much like being back home, with him and Mike Bloody Tennant creating what his mother called 'an atmosphere' whenever they were in the same room. Same hemisphere, more like. And not something he wanted to be reminded of.

'Fancy a walk, Tommy?'

'Wouldn't mind, but Orlando wants me to see if I can find that file on his laptop. If I bugger off instead he'll blow a sodding fuse. Maybe later.'

'OK . . .' Paul shrugged and watched Tommy leave the kitchen.

'I gotta go pick up some stuff, if you wanna get out.'

Paul frowned, looking to see where Sky's voice was coming from. 'Where are you?'

'Here.' A hand came up from behind one of the skip-rescue armchairs in the front room. The one with its back to him. 'Wanna go?'

'Yeah.'

Sky stood up and turned to look at Paul. 'Let's git, then.'

When Paul had asked where they were going, all Sky would say was 'the long way round', and they did just appear to be taking a leisurely afternoon walk to nowhere in particular. Which was, Paul decided, OK with him. He needed space to think. Everything seemed to be in limbo at the moment, nothing certain. He felt a bit like his life was spinning out of an orbit it had only just arrived in, that, as he was beginning to get used to living with these guys, actually being *in* Omega Place, Omega Place was starting to look very flaky.

'Why's it all gone so, I dunno, so *moody* back at the house, Sky?'

'You mean Terri and Rob, or you mean Orlando?'

'You can ignore Terri and Rob.'

Sky grinned. 'With practice.'

He carried on walking, and Paul waited to see if he would say any more, but he didn't. Thinking about it, all he really knew about Sky was that you never knew with him, could never work him out. He was a geezer, but he didn't behave that way; he was sort of irresponsible in a mature kind of way. And it was so odd being on friendly terms with a bloke older than his dad, being able to have a proper conversation without it ending up as an argument. Cos although his dad was all right, compared to the replacement model, he could still be a pain in the arse if he put his mind to it.

'What it is, is there's a bigger picture, man.'

'Sorry?' Paul wondered if he'd missed something Sky had said.

'There's a bigger picture than the one you guys see, and Lando's the only one can deal with it.'

'He's got you.'

'I don't do strategy.' Sky rolled himself a cigarette as he walked. 'Never did . . . I'm good on the ground. I put this thing together, been doing stuff like this a long time, but Lando's the one knows what to do with it.'

'What was it like?'

'What was what like?'

'My dad's always going on about when he was my age and how it was better and that.'

'And?'

'Well was it?'

Sky went into silent mode again, relighting his roll-up. 'It was different. And I think it often looks better from here, to those of us who were there at the time, because none of us likes change. But some of it really was better.'

'So how was it better, then?'

'The important thing, back then, was what you had to say. Everyone worth listening to had something to say . . . what does *anyone* today have to say? Really? It's all spin and bullshit . . . and everyone's so damn *passive*, like they don't care to believe in anything, anything at all. Not enough to get involved and do anything about it.'

'You mean like Omega Place?'

Sky nodded. 'Exactly like.' Then he shook his head. 'Back in the day everyone was doing stuff like this . . . questioning what was going on, not lying back and accepting it. Everyone *knew* what was worth getting out on the street for.'

'It's more complicated now, I reckon.'

'You know, it's not . . .' Sky stopped walking. 'Life *is* black and white, and like the man says, you don't need a weatherman to know which way the wind blows. There is right and there is wrong, Paul, and it only gets complicated because mine can be different to yours.'

30

Saturday 19th August, Kingsland Road

Things hadn't got much better by the time they got back to the house; from the moment Paul walked in he could tell nothing had really changed. There was still a tangible atmosphere, an undercurrent of resentment that hung around like a bad smell. He sighed, his shoulders slumping.

Sky patted him on the back. 'The joys of comradeship . . . you get good days and you get bad ones.'

'Go with the flow?'

'No point doing anything else, man.' Sky waved as he went upstairs. 'Some things you can't fight.'

Paul watched him go, presumably in search of Orlando, and stood for a moment, no idea what to do with himself; finally wandering off to see who else was around, he found Tommy in the kitchen, searching for a beer.

'You get the file back?'

'I wish.' Tommy closed the door to the cupboard he'd been rooting around in. 'Orlando's fit to be tied. Where'd you go?'

'Out . . . nowhere special. Just not here, you know?'

'Yeah, I do. I've got three sisters who all get their periods at the same time, and I don't know which is worse.'

'Are Terri and Rob still not talking?'

Tommy shook his head. 'Back on speaking terms.'

'What was that all about?'

'Rob tried to hit on her. Again.'

'He did?' Paul hoped he didn't sound too surprised, not wanting to let on he had no idea Rob had tried it on with Terri before. Not that he could honestly say he was surprised.

Tommy grinned. 'You can say one thing for that boy, he does not give up easily. I told him he'd got no chance, but he's convinced he can wear her down – and now that Izzy spends most of her time with Orlando, and Terri has a room to herself . . .' Tommy mimed sprucing himself up, '. . . off he went for another go, like.'

'When did he do that, then?'

'Last night, you were spark out.'

'What happened?'

'Not a lot. Crept out like a fox after chickens, came back with his tail between his legs and wouldn't tell me nothing. Terri did though, said she told him to stop listening to his dick, and piss off, and that he called her a lesbian.'

Paul grinned. 'Has that chat-up line ever worked for him before, then?'

'Doubt it, but one day, one of his attempts is gonna work and he's not going to have a clue what to do. He's always trying to punch well over his weight, that boy!'

'How old is he?'

'What would you say?'

'*He* said twenty, but I didn't believe him. Is he my age?'

'Rob's not even seventeen yet, man!' Tommy shook his head, laughing. 'He's a bloody child prodigy, and one of his many talents is lying through his teeth.'

'He's younger than *me*?'

'Yeah, but don't let on you know else he'll go mad with me . . .'

Paul had commandeered the bathroom after the evening meal – spaghetti and meat sauce cooked by Terri, with him given all the skivvy work, like chopping up onions and garlic and washing pots. He felt he needed space, even just an hour, on his own. He wasn't used to being around people all the time, and since arriving in London there really hadn't been a moment in the day, unless he was on the bog, when he wasn't with at least one other person.

There was enough hot water in the tank for a reasonable bath and, behind the locked door, he soaked until the water went tepid and his fingers turned into albino prunes. Staring at the cracked tiles on the walls, the peeling paintwork and the condensation beading on the ceiling he thought about Rob. About what it would be like to be him . . . because who *were* you if nothing in your life was real, if everything was a lie? And as Rob was always rewriting his own history, never admitting to a past, who *was* he? Paul stood up, shivering in the cooler air.

He wrapped his towel round him. The thing with Rob, he realised, was that, even though he might not know who he was, he sure as hell knew *what* he was. And to him that was all that mattered. Maybe he was right. Maybe it was all that mattered. What did he know? He had no real idea who *or* what Paul Hendry was. Even though he liked to think he'd cut himself loose and got away from where he came from, whatever happened, whatever he did, he'd always have somewhere to go back to. A starting point from which he could begin again.

Lucky bastard, he thought, drying himself off. And never

forget it.

There was no one in the bedroom when he went to get dressed. More quality time on his own. He was towelling his hair to get it a bit drier when the door flew open and Rob came bursting in.

'If I don't get out of here, man, I am gonna *strangle* someone! Honest, I am.'

Paul checked his watch as he put it on. Ten thirty-ish. 'Where you want to go?'

'Dunno. Anywhere. Somewhere.' Rob grinned manically at Paul. 'Coming then? Terri and me's going for a drink. Now. Here's doing my head in . . .' He grabbed his face with both hands to make his point clearer. 'Are you up for it?'

'What about Tommy and Sky, are they coming?'

'Nope, their answer is to stone themselves off the planet.' Rob turned and went out of the door, then came back. 'Was that a yes, cos we're off?'

'Give me a sec to put my shoes on . . .'

'Gone!'

Paul heard Rob thunder down the stairs as he shoved his trainers on, heard him yelling for Terri that they were off as he roughly tied the laces and grabbed his phone. And then, as he was about to leave the room, he spotted his Celtic ring and the chain with his shark's tooth, where he'd left them on the rickety bamboo table between his bed and Tommy's.

'Paul-eeeeee!'

Dithering, he turned to go back, then had second thoughts and left them where they were.

'Paul-eeeeeeeeee!'

Now that he knew how old Rob was his childishness seemed so much more blatant than before. Flicking the light switch off, Paul closed the door and ran for the stairs, taking them two and three at a time. The hall was in darkness – the bulb had gone a couple of days previously and no one had bothered to change it because they were supposed to be moving – and through the open front door he could see Rob and Terri waiting outside on the pavement. Paul grabbed his jacket from the pile hanging on the newel post at the end of the banister and joined them.

Rob dug around in his pocket and pulled out a bunch of flyers. 'We're going up West!'

'We want to go clubbing.' Terri took a couple of the flyers out of Rob's hand and waved them at Paul. 'Dance these shitty vibes out of our heads.'

'And we're not coming back till they're gone, right? You're up for that, aren't you, Pauly?'

'Too right I am . . . shame Tommy's not coming with us, though.'

'You can dance with us, Pauly!' Rob made a grab for Terri, who dropped the flyers and fended him off with an almost friendly punch.

As they walked off down the street, past some poor sod who had the bonnet up and was trying to fix the engine of his ratty old Escort van, Paul smiled to himself; Tommy was right, that boy did not give up easily.

Wiping his hands on a grease-stained oily rag, Dean Mayhew watched three of the four people in the photographs he'd been shown in the minimarket the night before as they turned the corner at the bottom of the road and disappeared. He bent back over the engine compartment of the van and carried on 'mending' it. He'd bought it for cash off some dodgy second-hand car dealer, right after he'd given the keys back to the estate agent.

He'd been in the street since just after 11.00 a.m., keeping the house under observation as best as one man on his own could without becoming totally obvious about it. He'd moved the van a couple of times, 'slept' a lot in the front passenger seat. In the afternoon he'd followed the older guy and his young mate for a bit, using a small high-gain mic that looked like a Bluetooth earpiece, in an unsuccessful attempt to see if he could glean anything interesting from their conversation.

From all his observations Dean was pretty sure there were now four people left in the squat: his target, Orlando, whom he'd yet to actually see, the dark-haired girl, the other crop-cut boy and the older man. And from what he'd overheard, the three who'd left weren't planning on coming back any time soon.

There'd been no sign at all of anyone else paying any attention to the house, so he was pretty sure that the opposition had yet to nail where Omega Place were operating from. In an area like this, people weren't that keen on talking to the law, didn't want to be seen snitching or turning anyone in. It could get you in trouble. If things continued to go his way, he'd be in, out and long gone before they ever found out where they should have been looking.

Dean picked up one of the flyers the girl had dropped. It was advertising something called *Dé-jà-vü* at a club in the West End and was just a list of names he didn't recognise and misspelt words; the chucking-out time, he noticed, was 2.00 a.m. What he had to do was only going to take minutes and he would leave it till about two o'clock as well. With any luck the clubbers would still be out and those in the house in a period of DOS. Deep Orthodox Sleep, when people were at their most unaware, when the body was at its most relaxed, when the heartbeat was at its slowest. That was the time to go to work.

31

Saturday 19th August, Tunbridge Wells

Henry Garden had spent a miserable day alone in his flat, smoking, drinking and fighting with his conscience. He was not a terrible person, not really. He would admit to being a man with a bad habit, maybe even bad habits, but that didn't make *him* bad. Unlucky, possibly; weak-willed, definitely.

But not evil.

Since he'd discovered the truth about Dean Mayhew, Garden had been on an emotional rollercoaster ride, swinging from abject shame at what his gambling had made him do, right over to the other extreme of incandescent rage at what Nick Harvey had made him do. Somewhere in the middle, a small part of him owned up to the fact that it was neither the gambling nor that bastard Harvey who was ultimately responsible. It was him.

If he kept his mouth shut and let matters take their course, whatever bad things happened would be his fault. And there was no denying, no way of glossing over the fact that something bad was definitely going to go down. Nick Harvey wanted the man he'd got running Omega Place dead, and if he did nothing that was what would happen.

Garden stared at the cordless handset lying on the table.

He checked the time: elevenish. He knew he should pick the phone up and call someone. Tell them what he knew so that there was a chance that Mayhew could be stopped. But, if he made that call, then his career was over. Everything he'd worked for, everything he was, would go up in smoke and he would be left exposed as the spineless coward behind the façade he'd spent years constructing and maintaining.

A lot of wine, and very little to eat, had, on the one hand, dulled Garden's reactions, slowing his world down. But, on the other hand, they'd dug down deep and exposed the raw nerves of his principles, his morality and his beliefs. Ethics that he'd been indoctrinated with, that had been driven into him at home and at school, but that years of public service had blunted and smothered. Political ethics . . . two mutually incompatible words, if there ever were ones.

His hand moved towards the phone . . .

32

Saturday 19th August, Thames House

They'd got their extra resources. More people, but more jobs to do. End result – just as overworked as before. A total SNAFU, as her father would say, although he'd cleaned it up by telling her it meant Situation Normal, All *Fouled Up*. Yeah, right . . . Mercer looked at her reflection in the window as she waited for a lift. A monochrome version of herself, drained of colour and running on empty, looked back; she stood up straighter and rotated her head, listening to the muscles in her neck creak, feeling the sharp pain as they twisted and remained as tense as ever. She tried to imagine a resolution, an end to this job – good or bad, right now she didn't care which – so it would all come to a stop and she could relax.

It was like walking a tightrope, waiting for the inevitable moment when you lost your balance and fell off, not knowing if there was a safety net below to catch you. Her brief had been to find these Omega Place people before anyone started taking too much notice of what they were doing – and, more to the point, what they were saying in their communications.

She knew she had a B-list soap star's colourful indiscretions – and a violent and very bloody civil disturbance in some godforsaken former Soviet republic – to thank for the fact that the press were otherwise engaged at the moment. But she was also very aware that her luck was not going to hold for ever. They'd had people all over the Kingsland Road area with photos since yesterday and, so far, a big fat nothing.

The lift arrived and she stepped in. As she pressed a button and watched the doors close she looked at her watch: eleven thirty on another Saturday night at the office. Her social life didn't deserve the description.

Mercer could hear a phone ringing in the office as she came down the corridor and she picked up her pace, running for the door. The ringing stopped just as her hand grabbed the handle and she swore, wondering whose call she'd missed and what it was about. Pushing the door open she went in to find Ray Salter sitting behind his desk, the phone jammed against his right ear by his shoulder. He'd obviously picked up her call and was nodding as he scribbled on the pad in front of him. She could see that whoever he was talking to, this wasn't a social call. Salter's face broke into a smile as he put the phone down.

'What is it, Ray?'

'We got 'em, boss!'

'Someone's come through for us?'

'Finally.' Salter pushed his chair back. 'They picked out all four of the pictures and have given up an address as well.'

'We'd better get a team together.'

'You want to go in tonight, boss?'

Mercer sat down at her desk. 'The sooner the better. I don't want them slipping through our fingers. What's the situation now, is anyone watching the place?'

'Yeah, but nothing too close, in case the targets get

spooked . . .' Salter indicated his phone. 'There's someone at each end of the street, apparently.'

'OK, good . . . do we have a plan of the house yet?'

Salter frowned and shook his head. 'Give us a chance, boss, I just took the call.'

'Right, right . . . but get on to that, will you? Until we know the layout we won't know how many people we should go in with. And tell Castleton to contact the duty officer and warn him that we're going to need an emergency issue of shooters and body armour.' Mercer picked up her phone, punched in a number and then put the receiver down. 'I'll email his BlackBerry . . .'

'Who?'

'Markham . . .' Mercer brought up the Outlook window on her computer and began typing a message to the Director of Internal Affairs. 'I want a record on the system of what we're planning. And I want official validation. Can't be too careful nowadays.'

'Let's hope he emails his reply.'

'With any luck he will . . .' Mercer looked over at Salter as she typed. 'What's the news about Henry Garden – anything incriminating?'

Salter shook his head. 'He's up to something, though. No one in his position leaves the office to make calls from public phone boxes, unless they *really* don't want the conversation monitored.'

Mercer sent the email and minimised the window. 'When was the last call?'

'Yesterday morning. He'd have had time to read the report about Bristol we had him specially copied in on.'

'Do we know who he was calling?'

'No. It was a mobile number, but we've not been able to

trace it to an owner.'

'Are you sure his people don't know we're interested in him?'

'We've been very careful.'

Mercer's computer *dinged* that she had incoming mail, which she immediately checked. It wasn't a reply from Alex Markham, and she looked away from the screen.

'I wonder who he's passing the information on to, and I wonder *why* he's doing it?'

'Might be a lifestyle glitch.'

'A what?'

'He lives on his own, in a nice part of Tunbridge Wells . . .'

'There's a nasty part?'

'I wouldn't know, boss, I'm just saying, the "bachelor" thing might have something to do with it.'

'Really?' God, Mercer thought, this job . . . the way it makes you think. 'You reckon it's blackmail, then?'

'What else?'

'Where is he now?'

'At home. Hasn't been out all day.'

As Salter picked up his phone, Mercer's computer *dinged* again, and this time it was a reply from Markham. She opened the mail, then sat back, smiling.

'We are to do, and I quote, "whatever needs to be done to expedite the situation". That would appear to be carte blanche, so let's get expediting.'

33

Saturday 19th August, Tunbridge Wells

Henry Garden sat looking at the phone, still there on the table an arm's reach away, exactly where it had been for the last hour. Was he *ever* going to find the courage to pick it up, or was he going to give in to his innate dread of being found out and just leave it where it was?

There was no other way he could paint the picture. He was acting like a total coward. Yellow, through and through.

And some little demon in his head kept dragging him, unwillingly, back to his school days. Bright, crystal-clear memories of that time repeatedly flashed in front of him; unwanted reminders of parallels he didn't want to consider. Being laughed at as he stood on the side of the swimming pool, not daring to dive in, gripped by the fear that he would smash his head open on the bottom and die horribly if he did; not standing by a friend, but turning tail and running away when they got into a fight; watching someone else get the blame – and, more importantly, the punishment – for a rash of thefts he'd been entirely responsible for.

They were all there. The small, pathetic and dirty little secrets were all coming back to haunt him tonight . . .

34

Sunday 20th August, Kingsland Road

Dean Mayhew checked his watch. 01:58:34. Time to go. He'd spent the last thirty minutes lying down right at the back of the shit-heap of a garden that belonged to the target house. Hidden in the darkness, waiting. Observing. He'd got there by going over the walls and through the back gardens of the houses at the rear, an unseen shadow, a silent but lethal ghost. Even the rats were keeping well away.

Then he was moving. Running quickly, keeping low to the ground, he zigzagged towards the back door of the house; reaching its shadows, he snapped on a pair of thin latex gloves. The lock kept him out for all of seven seconds and then he was inside, standing motionless in the kitchen, letting his eyes adjust, sniffing the air and listening to the house and what it was telling him. He could smell dope and he could hear someone's breathing, quite nearby.

His watch said it was now 02:02:05. Enough pissing about. Dean unholstered his .45 automatic pistol, took the suppressor out of its pocket in his black denim jacket and screwed it on to the barrel. He pulled the slide back, chambered a round and cocked the weapon, the perfectly maintained parts making almost no sound as they meshed. Now he was ready. Checking all safeties were off, he moved out of the kitchen and into the room where the deep, regular breathing was coming from.

The aroma of dope was stronger, but in the gloom he couldn't yet see where the sleeping person was. With the Glock 21, now almost fifteen inches long with its silencer attached, hanging by his side, Dean skirted the furniture and finally saw the prone figure. Slumped in one of the armchairs, legs right out in front of him, was the older man. Dead to the world. Dean considered making his condition a permanent one, but that wasn't part of his brief and he saw no reason to waste the bullets. The man was so wasted he wasn't going to wake up, but, if he was unfortunate enough to do so, and he got in the way, it would be for the last time . . .

02:04:19. He backed out of the room and entered the hallway, stopping to listen again. Nothing. He took out a small Maglite torch, turned it on and inspected the stairs; covered in threadbare carpeting, they were going to squeak like mice, more than likely, but if he kept to the wall side and took them three steps at a time he should make the minimum amount of noise . . .

02:05:01. Dean stood on the first-floor landing. Four doors and a staircase going up another floor. Door one: bathroom; door two: boxroom, empty, smell of dope; door three: twin bedroom, empty, perfume; door four: two beds and a camp bed, one bed occupied by the sleeping figure of the other crop-cut boy. The air was rank with sweat, aftershave, beer and feet. Just like the army . . .

02:06:48. The door to the loft room at the top of the next set of stairs was closed. Behind it must be his target. And, as she was nowhere else, the second girl. Tough break for her, if she was serious about this man, but that was the way it went sometimes. Dean turned the door handle and

214

very carefully pushed it open a foot or so; slipping into the room he saw two figures on the double mattress on the floor.

He took the photo Nick had given him out of his pocket and checked it against the sleeping man, lying on his back with his mouth half open. He was older and had less hair, his glasses were on the book by the bed, but it was him. Curled up next to him, one arm thrown over his chest, the dark-haired girl he'd seen in the back garden was smiling in her sleep. Well, at least he wasn't going to die alone. The smallest of mercies . . .

02:07:23. Dean moved round so the ejected cartridge cases would fall where he could find them easily and brought the Glock up so it was half an inch from the man's forehead. This, he thought to himself as he sighted, braced his right wrist and prepared to pull the trigger twice in quick succession, was a direct consequence of not doing as you were told.

THEWW . . . THEWW . . .

The sound – 'soft, like the breath of an angry angel', as someone he knew had once described it – escaped as the suppressor did its job, instantly reducing the pressure and cooling the gases blown out after the two bullets exited the barrel.

02:07:56. Scrambled brains for breakfast, Dean thought as he glanced at the girl to see if she was going to stir, but she didn't. Picking up the two expelled cartridge cases, he tucked them, still warm, in the back pocket of his jeans, left the room and shut the door behind him. Job done. Money in the bank. He stood on the stairs for a moment and listened. Again, nothing, just house noises. He carried on down, gripping the silencer in his left hand as he crossed the landing, about to start unscrewing it, but then thinking no, maybe not. He wasn't away quite yet . . .

As the thought crossed Dean's mind, the door to his left opened; Dean looked over his shoulder to find the crop-haired boy standing there in a creased, beer-stained T-shirt and his boxers, weaving slightly from side to side. Not asleep any more.

The boy frowned and you could almost hear his brain attempting to work out what was going on.

'Who the fu . . . wha the . . . ?'

His voice was loud in the silence. Unacceptably loud, for Dean's purposes. He'd have to shut him up.

'Oi, you . . . I said, like, din't I . . . right?' The boy stumbled out of the room, pointing at him.

Dean crossed the landing in two strides, grabbed the boy's shoulder and spun him sharply round and slammed him into the wall. 'Shut it!' he whispered in the boy's ear, smelling the dope and the alcohol he was sweating out. 'Shut-it-right-up . . .'

He raised his right hand and was about to use the gun butt to turn the kid's lights out when he lurched backwards, his fists flailing, and Dean had to quickly step out of his way.

'Don'cha tell *me* wha'a fu-in do!'

Dean glanced at his watch. 02:09:11. This was not how it was supposed to be going. Not. At. All. This bloody drunken kid was screwing everything up, making a mess of all his timings! It was almost like a switch had been flicked in his head and the control program taken offline. Dean went all the way from 'chilled' to 'ballistic' in one breath. The boy went from standing to eating the carpet in the same length of time.

'You stupid . . .' One knee on the boy's spine, and holding him down by the neck, Dean placed the silenced barrel at the base of the kid's skull, fired twice and stood up. Then he fired once more. '. . . little shit.'

In the quiet he took a deep, deep breath, inhaling the sweet smell of combat; he loved the fumes of battle, even a crap little fight like this. Dean could feel a calmness descending on him as his anger faded and the feral beast side of his nature retreated to whatever part of his brain that it hid in. Waiting to be let out again.

As he watched the dark liquid pool around the boy's head he saw the crucifix he was wearing on a thin gold chain round his neck. Reaching down, he yanked the chain and it broke.

'Not much use, was it?' he muttered, throwing it into the shadows.

Dean stood, reassessing his situation. Two people still left alive in the house who could possibly cause him trouble. Ten bullets left. The maths worked out OK. He checked his watch again as he bent down to pick up the shell cases. 02:09:49. He was overrunning, and it was definitely time he got out of this place.

35

Sunday 20th August, Leicester Square, London

It had been good to get out of the house. Be on the street, but not have to think about flyering or stickering or getting caught smashing some piece of equipment or being scared shitless you were going to fall and get smashed yourself. Walking to the bus stop with Rob and Terri Paul'd really felt a part of Omega Place, part of something that was doing important stuff, *really* important. He believed they were forcing people to look at who was looking at them. You had to make that kind of noise, like Orlando said, otherwise the public just acted like children and got led around by the nose, thinking that everything politicians did was in their best interests.

As they'd waited for a bus, Paul had watched the people walking by. They had to be told, but you also had to have a good time *some*time, else you'd get totally like . . . well, totally like Orlando, and who wanted to be like that? Not him. Not the others, either. And not tonight, when they were going to have a *laugh*. He could do with a laugh.

Paul hadn't had this much fun, ever. Not ever. Everything had been a gas, starting with finding that he'd picked up the wrong jacket when he'd left the house and was wearing Tommy's. Had Tommy's wallet and everything! And you could say what you liked about Rob, but he knew how to have a good time, and he was mad, mad, *bad* mad company. Did not care *what* he did or *what* he said. But then Paul pretty much knew that about him already. He just hadn't seen him in action, out on the town kind of thing.

Him and Rob and Terri had been to a couple of bars and one club, possibly two. They'd been thrown out of one of the clubs because Rob had bothered some girls. Apparently. He said he'd just asked them to dance. Terri said he'd probably tried to slip his tongue down their throats when he was doing the asking.

Anyway. Whatever. It didn't matter because it was two o'clock and they were now at some all-night caff near Leicester Square, eating kebabs with chilli sauce, drinking Coke float, with extra vodka that Terri had got from somewhere or other, and they were rerunning everything they'd just done, surrounded by loads of other people doing *exactly* the same thing. How weird was that? Truly weird, but a hell of a lot better than being back at the house, they all agreed about that. Tonight was not a night for being shut away. It was a night for doing things you were going to regret the next day, but couldn't care less about at the time.

Like trying to snog Terri.

Actually, *not* that. Some small, but vitally important part of Paul's head that had to do with survival had still been aware enough to know that he wouldn't have to wait till the morning to very much regret doing that. Unlike Rob. But then Rob appeared to have the attention span of a goldfish and never learnt from his mistakes. Just got better at making them. Terri had punched his face out when he'd tried to kiss her a second time, but nothing got broken and Rob was drunk enough to think it was very funny, the way girls punched, so everything was still A-OK, as his dad said.

His dad . . .

Paul wondered what he was doing on this Saturday-night-Sunday-morning. He'd been gone now almost a month. Would his dad even know? Would his mam have told him he'd run off? Maybe, if she could find a way of making it look like it was his dad's fault. But probably not, because she wouldn't want his dad to be able to blame the replacement. Oh no.

God, how hard was it to get on with people? You should be able to get on with the ones you knew best, ferchrissake, as you had the most practice with them. But that never seemed to be the case, leastways, not with anyone he knew back home. It seemed you liked the people best who were your friends, not your family. But then you could leave friends behind, say about someone 'they were my friend, once'. But you never could do that with family. Family were for ever and you couldn't say 'he was once my dad'. You might want to, but you couldn't.

Paul realised he'd kind of zoned out long enough for the ice cream in his glass to melt completely. Rob, who was attempting to chat up some foreign students at the next table, seemed not to have noticed, but Terri was smiling at him across the table as she constructed another cigarette.

'You were miles away.' She licked the paper and rolled. 'Anywhere nice?'

'Home.'

'Where the heart is? Some girlfriend you left behind when you followed me down?'

Paul felt himself blush. 'No . . . thinking about me dad.'

Terri flicked her lighter. 'If I never see mine again it'll be too soon.'

There was no answer to that, Paul reckoned, so he kept his trap shut, not wanting to say the wrong thing. He looked out of the café window and hoped there would never be a time when he felt like that about his own dad.

36

Sunday 20th August, Kingsland Road

Dean Mayhew liked to think of himself as a kind of an alternative, twenty-first-century Buddhist. He believed that all existence was suffering. And that most of the cause of the suffering was desire. Certainly it was true that, for him, not getting what he wanted caused both him and the person not giving it to him pain. Buddhists also believed that freedom from suffering was nirvana, which was attained through ethical conduct, wisdom and mental discipline; Dean believed he could tick all those boxes. While he knew that his ethics were not those most people would understand, he stuck to them like tin to a magnet; he was very wise in the ways of the world he lived in and his mental discipline was awesome . . . unless he lost his temper. After all, no one was perfect.

Looking down at the floor he felt a momentary spike of regret, a tiny, instantly forgettable pinprick on his scarred conscience, for what he'd done to the crop-haired boy; but you would never attain nirvana if you didn't move on. Onwards and upwards. He was about to scoop up the three ejected shell cases when there was a massive blow that shook the house, and then the front door, the bottom of which he could just see from where he was standing, flew inwards. Glass and wood splinters everywhere.

Moments like this were what he'd been trained for. Instant assessment of the unfolding situation; likely outcomes; best advised actions; worst-case scenarios. All this in the time it would take most people to fill their pants.

This was not a bomb. It was most probably a steel two-man battering ram, which meant that either bailiffs had got a lot more proactive, or the other lot had found the house too. The likely outcome of which was that the place should be surrounded, except he hadn't heard any entry noises from the rear of the house, so someone was being a bit sloppy. And that meant his best and only action, if he wanted his life to carry on pretty much as it had been, had to be a swift and speedy retreat. Which was when the two men carrying the ram came into view, silhouettes backlit by the street lamps.

Dean wasn't out to kill now, just disable. Put out of action. Tie up other personnel who would have to attend to their injured colleagues. These people would be wearing upper-body armour, so leg shots were what you went for.

Even if they'd looked up they wouldn't have seen the shadowy face-blackened figure kneeling on the landing. By the time they saw the muzzle flashes it would be too late. And so, as they stopped in the hallway, each man in turn had no idea why one of his legs felt like it'd been hit by something deliriously hot, and was then whipped out from underneath him as he collapsed, writhing on the floor.

Dean stood, turned and stepped over the body on the landing, pushing open the bathroom door. In his mind's eye he ran over the schematic of the house that he'd roughed out as he'd gone from room to room . . . the bathroom was over the kitchen, and the kitchen had a pitched-roof extension just below the bathroom window . . . which he now sprinted straight towards. He only had the space to take three short steps, but it should be enough.

Head down, forearms up, covering his face to take the brunt of the action, pistol in his right hand, barrel extension tucked tight into his armpit, Dean gave one final push and launched himself at the window. He smashed through the glass and thin wooden dividers, turning the leap into a fly-ing somersault . . . one complete turn and up on to his feet, knees bent and then powering upwards as he jumped off the roof and out into the blackness at the rear of the house.

He knew this was the riskiest part of the whole business. A real, no-shit leap in the dark. The garden was a dump, rubble and crap everywhere, so who knew what he'd land on. Whatever it was, it was not going to be soft. The ground rushed towards him, a grey blur that resolved itself into broken furniture, discarded junk and bottles as he landed on it. Dean tried to fall as protectively as he could, and he did a good job, considering, but there was no way to stop himself from stumbling and falling to his left as he tried to start running.

Broken glass dug into him, sharp teeth trying to bite his hand as he pushed himself back up, the piece that dug into his palm making him drop the Glock so he could pull it out. No way he could go back to get it, but while he hated leav-ing expensive gear in the field, they'd get nothing off it, no prints, no serial number. Behind him Dean could hear the sound of people busting out of the house, coming after him. He knew, whoever they were, they weren't likely to be combat-seasoned and they'd still be shaken by what had happened in the house; which, hopefully, would give him the time he needed to get over the fence before they started getting organised.

Standing in what passed for the back garden of the squat, Jane Mercer snapped her phone shut. The chopper with the heat-seeking gear and mega spotlight was up and would be overhead within minutes, but whether that would be soon enough she had her doubts. The individual who'd been in the house when they went through the door was no amateur, that much was obvious.

The two men who were down had each been taken out by a single shot to the leg by someone who knew not only what to target, but how to hit what he wanted in almost total darkness. While there was no way she could have known anything like this was going to happen, no possible way she could have planned for it, this was not going to look good on the report. Neither was the fact that there were two dead bodies in the place, and the person who'd killed them had got away.

Mercer looked down at the fence he must've gone over. There was blood on it, Ray Salter had told her, and the man had dropped his gun; he was lucky all he'd done was cut himself, jumping off that roof. But this had been a professional hit, and somebody was picking up the tab, which wouldn't be cheap, so luck probably had nothing to do with it. She wondered who the hell the man was, who'd sent him and why.

The house was secured now and she'd called for back-up. Right now it was just her and the team, but very soon there'd be Scene of Crime, the body boys and whoever else thought they should be involved. Mercer, who wanted time with the two live ones they'd got before anyone else poked their noses in, went back inside.

Walking through the kitchen she found Ray Salter in the

front room with the older man she recognised from the High Street Ken and Bristol surveillance footage. Upstairs Castleton and one of the newly seconded female team members were looking after the hysterical girl who'd been found with the dead body at the top of the house, waiting for the medical unit to arrive so someone could sedate her. The man merely seemed bemused, sitting, handcuffed, in the armchair he'd been found slumped in; he was frowning, with a puzzled expression on his face.

'What's your name, sir?'

The man looked up. 'Scuse me?'

American accent . . . Mercer's turn to be surprised. 'Your name, what is it?'

'Sky . . . you know, like "kiss the sky"?' The man laughed. 'Hendrix, man, he could play . . . right? Like a damn demon . . .'

Mercer looked at Salter, who jerked a thumb at an ashtray on the floor by the chair, and the bong next to it. She nodded.

'Just your name, sir, that's all we want. Then we can start processing you out of here.'

The man nodded and smiled as he scratched his head, which, Mercer thought, made him look like a wasted Stan Laurel.

'I tole you, it's Sky, man!' He shifted in the chair and made like he was trying to get to the back pocket of his jeans. 'You let me get my wallet, I'll show you . . .'

'Stay still, sir,' Mercer looked at Salter. 'He's been searched, right?'

'Yeah, boss . . . the wallet's there on the box.' Salter pointed at the large cardboard box that was obviously used as a table. Mercer reached down, picked up the wallet and began looking through it.

The man looked amazed. 'You got my wallet – how'd you do that? Didn't feel a *thing*! Great trick, man!'

The wallet was old and well-used, the leather soft and slightly greasy, moulded to the shape of the back pocket it must have spent years in. Tucked away in one of its credit card slots Mercer found a small, laminated card with a photograph of a much younger version of the man on it. It was a Wisconsin driver's licence, with a Milwaukee address, and it belonged to a Jerome M. Petersen. It had been issued in 1966.

37

Sunday 20th August, Kingsland Road

03:10. An hour in and the squat was now the property of the white romper-suited Scene of Crime boys and the kind of senior officials who specialised in appearing, well after the shit had stopped hitting the fan, to 'take charge'. Sidelined for the moment by internal bureaucracy, Mercer was in the kitchen, with her team; it was still their gig and they weren't going to bow out that easily.

'OK,' Mercer pulled out a chair and sat down at the table, 'what do we have? Who's got the timeline?'

'Me,' Perry waved his notepad. 'Want to go through it now, boss?'

Mercer nodded. 'Better that we're all singing off the same song sheet, right?'

Perry sat down and flipped his pad open. 'We rammed the door at approximately 02:10 hours, me and Tony following the muscle, so's we could get straight through the ground floor and secure the rear of the building. But Phillips and Young got hit almost immediately; I think I saw the muzzle flash, but whoever was up there on the first landing was using a silenced weapon. We had two officers down and Tone and me pulled them out of the way as Ray and you,' Perry nodded at Mercer, 'went through after us, Ray up the stairs and you to the back. The shooter went out of the bathroom window about a minute and a half in, and was over the rear fence and away by the time you got the kitchen door open.

'I called for back-up and medical assist at about 02:12 hours and did what I could for Phillips and Young, who both had nasty leg wounds; Ray secured the ground floor. In the front room he found Jerome Petersen, so stoned he'd slept through everything; on the first landing Tony and back-up found the first body, three shots to the back of the head. They went on up and discovered the girl and the second vic. He had two shots to the temple. Back-up started to arrive at about 02:45 hours.'

'Thanks, John.' Mercer sat back. 'Opinions?'

'A pro hit, boss, SAS trained.' Ray Salter lit a cigarette. 'Wouldn't you say?'

Mercer raised her eyebrows and nodded in assent. 'Trouble with those types is you can't *un*train them . . . and what was he using, Ray?'

'The weapon we found in the garden was a .45 calibre Glock; the wounds are consistent with him using hollow-point ammunition. Small hole going in, big one going out. Guaranteed end result. The kid lost his face, and our guys were lucky he didn't hit anything major . . . lost a lot of blood as it was.'

'Why d'you think the kid got it worse than – what did our American friend call him, Ray?'

'Who, the man upstairs?' Mercer nodded. 'He called him Orlando, boss. Orlando Welles.'

'Right, Orlando. Any sign there was someone called James Baker here?'

'No, boss, not so far.'

'Any news yet on the prints from the body?'

229

Salter shook his head. 'Waiting for a call.'

'So why did the boy warrant the extra treatment, d'you think?'

'No idea, yet.' Salter flicked some ash into the sink. 'Evidence says he was sleeping in a room with two other people, both male from the looks of it. I think we have a line on who he is though.'

'How?'

'There was just the one jacket hanging at the bottom of the stairs, and it's the right size to fit him. The Yank said it wasn't his, and it's not the girl's because the wallet I found in it belongs to someone called Paul Thomas Hendry, seventeen, from just outside Newcastle, according to his driving licence. And there were some other personal effects by the bed he'd been sleeping in, a ring and a kind of shark's tooth thing on a chain that could be his.'

'Seventeen . . . sweet Jesus . . .' Mercer got up. 'Do we know who the girl who was with this Orlando is?'

Salter ran the cold tap on his dog end and put it into an empty milk carton on the work surface. 'The girl's called Isabel Morley, boss . . . didn't get much else out of her as she was totally freaked, waking up next to a dead boyfriend, then seeing the mess on the landing. We couldn't get her out of the house without her clocking there was another body.'

'You didn't cover it?'

'Course we did, but a body under a sheet's still a body. No way of getting round that. The girl had hysterics when she saw it.'

'The job was to off this Orlando character, wasn't it?' Mercer stared out of the kitchen window, not asking anyone in particular. 'That was the neat, tidy, professional shot,

230

right? The boy was a mistake; he was in the wrong place at the very worst time, poor sod. Glad I'm not going to be the one telling his parents.'

Salter lit another cigarette. 'Let's hope they give a shit . . .'

Tony Castleton, Ray Salter and one of the CID blokes had gone to a nearby all-night shop to restock with cigarettes, John Perry was with the Scene of Crime boys, going over what they'd found so far, and Jane Mercer was sitting by herself in the kitchen, thinking they should probably call it a day. Thinking, maybe on her way home she'd swing by the station Petersen and the girl had been taken to. And then her mobile went.

She picked up without checking the number and found herself talking to Alex Markham. Thrown for a second, she didn't know what to say; he was the last person she'd expect to be calling her now.

'Sir?'

'I gather the operation didn't go quite as planned.'

'Not quite, sir.' Bad news, she thought, always travels fast. 'We disturbed someone else's operation . . . two dead, two of ours down, and I'm afraid he got away, sir.'

'Bad timing.'

'Sorry, sir?'

'I had a call, about an hour ago. Too late, I'm afraid, for it to be of any use to you.'

Mercer stood up, the tiredness she'd been wearing like a cloak falling off her shoulders as she started to pace the kitchen. 'A call about this operation?'

'In a manner of speaking.'

'Who from, sir?'

'Henry Garden. I gather you've had him under surveillance.'

'We think he had some kind of connection to Omega Place, sir . . . that he was probably the source of the RPA info.'

'Well, you thought right. And he also confessed to passing on information about the Bristol operation, and the general whereabouts of the squat.'

'Information?' Mercer stopped walking. 'Why would he give them information about themselves?'

'He didn't. Garden gave it to the person who's apparently been funding Omega Place, and *he* apparently gave it to someone called Dean Mayhew.'

Mercer changed ears. 'Dean Mayhew? Not a name we've come across so far . . . who is he?'

'He was the one who shot your people.'

Mercer wasn't at home in bed. She was back at the office, with the rest of the team, and she felt like she was operating entirely thanks to adrenalin and caffeine. The former was running out and the latter wasn't really having much effect any more. Dog-tired didn't really describe her condition.

'What d'you think of this, Ray?' She tapped the copy of the transcript of Garden's phone call on the desk in front of her.

'I think his timing was crap.' Salter picked up a sheet of paper. '"*I've been battling with my conscience all day*" . . . bullshit, he could've made that call the moment he worked out who the info was being given to; he just didn't have the guts to do it, so two people died and two of ours got shot. Where is he now?'

'Downstairs, being taken apart.'

'What about . . .' Salter referred to the transcript, '. . .

232

Nicholas Harvey?'

'Ditto. He was brought in kicking and screaming his inno-
cence, threatening the arse off everybody in sight with
major legal action, but it's all over. Garden's done his fat
lady impression.'

'Will he get immunity for giving evidence?'

Mercer shook her head. 'Didn't ask, did he? No bargaining,
just cracked and spilled the beans.'

'Good. I hate it when creeps like him get let off easy.'
Salter's phone rang and he picked up, listening and nodding and then putting the handset back down. 'Tony, boss.'

'What's he say?'

'Fingerprints are back. Orlando Welles is none other than –'

'James Hudson Baker?'

'Hole in one. And the US State Department has confirmed
the identity of Jerome Petersen . . . He is who his docu-
ments say he is, and his name is still flagged and tagged,
apparently.'

'Why, what'd he do?' Mercer picked up her coffee cup, and
then realised all it contained was an inch or so of cold
dregs.

'He was a dope dealer, got busted with "a significant
quantity of primo home-grown" I was told, and jumped bail.
Told the Canadian authorities he was a draft dodger, then
disappeared.'

'And managed to get into the UK, somehow.'

'Looks like it.' Salter picked up a ballpoint and started
doodling cage-like constructions on his copy of the Henry
Garden phone transcript. 'I wonder if we'll have to give him
back before he goes to trial. Could be better for him if we
didn't, right?'

Mercer shrugged. 'I'm too tired to care . . . did Tony say

233

anything about this Dean Mayhew character? Do we have a line on him yet, where he might be?'

'No . . .' Salter leaned back in his chair, rubbing his eyes. 'He's hurt, but we don't know how bad, and, even though he dropped a weapon, that's no guarantee he's not still armed. I'd lay good money that he is.'

'He'll have gone to ground . . .' Mercer drained her cup of cold black coffee. 'That's what they do; he'll wait for the dust to settle, then make his move.'

'We going to put his face out?'

'If we do, it won't be for this.' Mercer shuffled the transcript. 'This will never have happened.'

38

Sunday 20th August, Kingsland Road

Paul couldn't remember exactly when they'd finally decided to go home. Whenever it was, Rob – big surprise – had been up for more, but Paul hadn't been too unhappy when Terri'd said she was calling it a day as she remembered hearing Orlando say to Sky something about an early start. He did look at his watch when the night bus dropped them off, saw that it was just after half past three and thought that he was going to feel like shit if an early start really was on the cards.

It was as they came nearer to the road the squat was in that Paul noticed the normal night-time activity in the area – when the shadows came out to play, as Sky put it – was somehow different. More edgy. More sirens, if that was possible. He followed Terri and Rob into a twenty-four-hour minimarket for one of Rob's emergency snack purchases, watching as an unmarked Mondeo, with a flashing light on its dashboard, accelerated down the street.

'Wonder what's going on tonight?'

Rob didn't even look up from his trawl of the sweet shelves. 'Drugs bust, what else, man?'

'Come on, Rob, get a move on, I'm knackered!' Terri was flicking through the magazines, looking very like she had when Paul had followed her into the newsagent near the train station, all that time ago. All those miles away.

'They had your pitchers, them lot.'

Paul turned towards the bloke behind the counter; not much older than him, if at all, looking totally foreign, with a completely London accent. He noticed Terri and Rob had stopped what they were doing and were staring at the bloke, too.

Rob walked over. 'What was that, mate?'

'Yesterday, innit? This geezer come in with some shots for us to look at, say if we knew where the people in them lived? They was of you.' He nodded at all three of them. 'Straight up.'

Terri came up to the counter. 'What did you say?'

The young guy backed away slightly. 'Me? Nuffin. Why would I, right?'

'But you could tell it was us?'

'Course I could.' He jabbed a finger at Rob. 'Chocolate Boy's in here all the time, innit.'

'What did the person with the photos want, Abdul?' Rob thumped a kingsize Mars bar on the counter as if it was a deadly weapon.

'Leave it out, Rob . . .' Terri made a calming motion with her hand.

'Leave what out? He *is* Abdul, it's his name . . . we're mates, OK?' Rob smiled at Abdul and they touched knuckles. 'What were they after, like?'

'Wanted t'know if you was living round here, bruv. He din't come on like plod, but I could tell that's what he was, the geezer.' Abdul glanced out of the shop window. 'And I think it looks like he found someone who told him . . .'

'Why?'

Abdul jerked a thumb out of the window. 'Your road's bin

like Piccadilly bleeding Circus for the last hour or so . . . vans, ambulances and stuff, *and* they've had a helicopter up an all. One of those with the chunky spotlight?'

The hairs on the back of Paul's neck bristled and all the moisture was sucked right out of his mouth. What the hell was going on? Sure, what they were doing wasn't legal, but was it worth *this* much police activity? It was like they were terrorists . . . he looked over at Rob and Terri for some kind of guidance as to how he should be feeling, or what he should be doing, but neither of them seemed to know what was going on either.

'You wanna crash upstairs, guys?'

All three of them looked at Abdul.

'Well, you can't hardly go home, can you?'

Rob put some money on the counter, picked up his Mars bar and stripped off the wrapper. 'What's upstairs?'

'Store room. You can kip on the floor there, till I go off.'

'When's that?' Rob asked through a mouthful.

'Round sevenish, when me uncle Mahmoud comes in to take over. I'll have to chuck you out before that.'

Terri moved back from the counter as another car with a flashing light sped past the shop. 'Why are you doing this?'

'Me?'

'Yeah, you.'

'I told you . . .' Rob stuffed the last of the bar into his mouth. 'He's my mate, that's why.'

Abdul nodded, picking up the money on the counter and chucking it in the till. 'You don't trust me, you don't got to stay, sister.'

'I'm not . . .'

'We'll stay, Ab . . . OK?' Rob looked pointedly from Terri to Paul.

'Yeah.' Paul nodded, unable to think what else to do, aware that the power dynamic had subtly switched from Terri to Rob. 'Right . . .'

'Terri?' Rob looked at her.

She smiled a tight, humourless smile back at him, then shot a glance at Abdul. 'Thanks.'

The room was packed, floor to ceiling, with boxes. Crisps, toilet cleaner, baked beans, Cuppa Soup, washing powder, Pot Noodles, instant coffee, dog food, tights. All the necessities, everything you might, for some reason, need at any time of the day or night.

Paul stood by one of the windows that looked out on to the street below. The bottom half was broken, the hole, and most of the glass, covered with a piece of cardboard, the top half just filthy. Through the city grime he could see the end of their road. Could just make out the diagonal stripes on the rear of a police patrol car. There hadn't been any activity for a few minutes, but he couldn't drag himself away. What had happened to the others . . . what was going to happen to him?

'Sit down, Paul. Get some rest, we're gonna be back out on the street in a couple of hours.'

Paul looked down at Terri, sitting on the floor of the darkened room in a shaft of street light; beside her was the slumped figure of Rob, curled up, fast asleep.

'How does he do that?'

'He doesn't care.'

'About what?'

'Anything.'

Paul sat down opposite Terri. 'What are we going t'do, then . . . when we leave here?'

'Us?'

'Yeah, us.'

Terri looked away. 'I don't think there *is* an "us" any more, Pauly. If they got Orlando and Sky, that's it. Game over.'

They? Game over? *What?* Paul closed his eyes and tried to slow his head down, tried to think. Think. Think. Think. It was hard to do, with everything collapsing around him . . . if the squat had been raided – and what else could all the cops mean? – then what he had with him, the clothes he was dressed in and the stuff in his pockets, that was it. Everything he owned. And the jacket wasn't even his.

And, to top it all, in an hour or so, Abdul would be turfing them out into a street where people – no, get real, not people – where the *police* were looking for them. Had their pictures. Knew what they looked like. Paul still couldn't believe the huge amount of activity there was going on just to bust the squat. A helicopter, what was that all about?

Paul opened his eyes. 'What's going on, Terri?'

'How the hell should I know?'

'They must've got Orlando and the others, right?'

Paul stared at Terri, who was looking anywhere but at him. 'I told you,' she mumbled. 'I don't know, OK?'

'This raid's about Omega Place, and they're acting like we've got bombs and shit.' He stood up and went to look out of the window again; the police car seemed to have gone. 'Why are we hanging round here?'

'Stop asking me questions like I've all the bloody answers, will you?'

Terri's raised voice woke up Rob, who rolled over on to his back and yawned. 'What's up . . . lovers' tiff?'

'Piss off, Rob.'

'Charming . . .' Rob sat up, rubbing his face. 'Feel like

239

I've eaten bleeding cat litter.'

Before either Terri or Paul could think of an appropriate reply, the door to the store room opened and Abdul came in.

'Heads up, guy.'

Rob stood up. 'What?'

'I just had a couple or three of them plain-clothes geezers in the shop.'

'Looking for us?'

'Nah, getting fags an stuff, bruv.'

'So?'

'So they was just outside the shop, stopped to spark up, and I heard what they said, din't I? Thought you'd wanna know.'

Terri got up off the floor and brushed her jeans down. 'What did they say, Abdul?'

'One goes something like, "D'you know the ID of the bodies yet?" and the other geezer says . . .'

'*Bodies?*' Terri's eyes widened.

'Yeah, bodies, and the other geezer says that, like, the one shot in the top room's called Orlando, and they think the kid's probably called Paul sunnink or other. And then they pissed off and I din't hear no more.' Abdul looked at his watch. 'My uncle'll be here in a half hour or so, right?'

Rob nodded. 'We'll be down, OK?'

'Later.'

The three of them said nothing as they watched the store-room door close. They stayed silent as what Abdul had said sank into their tired brains and they tried to make sense of it.

Terri sat down, head in her hands. 'Orlando's dead, been shot?'

240

'But . . .' Rob frowned. 'Didn't Abdul say the other one was . . . ?'

'Me?' Paul looked out of the window at the empty street below. 'Yeah, Abdul said the other body was me.'

'OK, OK . . .' Rob frowned at Paul. 'But why'd they think . . .'

Paul turned away from the window. 'Must be the jacket, mustn't it?' He pulled at the one he was wearing like it was clinging to him. 'Remember? I took Tommy's by mistake? So he must be dead, too. Why would anyone kill him, ferchrissake? Who'd ever want Tommy dead?'

39

Monday 21st August, King's Cross, London

Paul sat on his own at a table in the rear of the nearly empty café, as far away from the window as possible. Rob had gone to the toilet and Terri was off getting some tobacco and papers. A couple of minutes back he'd thought about pinching himself very hard, just to test whether this was all really happening, or if he was, by some miracle, actually asleep and dreaming. But though this might all seem like a nightmare, he knew he was awake.

He was awake. And he was alive. But Tommy and Orlando were dead and Sky and Izzy were banged up somewhere in police custody. He could not believe it was true, that he'd never see Tommy again. How was that possible? Who the hell had allowed that to happen? He didn't live in a world where people he knew got *killed*, ferchrissake! He didn't.

He'd left home not knowing what he was looking for and by accident he'd found a weird kind of other family, which had taken him in and accepted him for what he was, taught him to think, taught him that you needed action *and* words. Whatever you thought about Orlando, he could see the big picture, made you look at it and see what was *really* happening. And now, now he was lost again, the family had been destroyed, Orlando was gone and it was just the three of them.

Paul sat at the table, silent and still, not knowing if he felt scared or whether it was anger laced with fear that was making it impossible for him to think straight. He stopped staring blankly at the table and looked up. Terri and Rob had been gone a long time and a sudden empty feeling in the pit of his stomach made him think they weren't coming back, that they'd made some kind of plan behind his back and had pissed off and left him. Then the door to the café opened and Terri walked in, smiling at him, and Rob appeared at the table, wiping his hands on his jeans.

Rob sat next to Paul, grinning. 'I needed that!'

'We didn't need to know.' Terri took a folded newspaper out of the carrier bag she'd got with her, put it on the table and turned away. 'I'll get us some more teas . . . and it doesn't look like we made the papers.'

Paul grabbed the tabloid, checking the headlines on the first half dozen or so pages. 'There's nothing . . . not a word.' He was whispering, even though there was no one near enough to hear what he said. 'How can two people being shot dead *not* be a story?'

Rob shrugged. 'Dunno, mate.'

'Don't you care?'

'About not being in the papers? No. Less said the better, know what I mean?'

'They're going to cover it all up, aren't they? No one's ever going to know what happened to them . . .' Paul wasn't whispering now. 'Bastards!'

Terri sat down opposite Paul. 'Keep your voice down, OK?'

'But –'

'But nothing. I don't know *why* there's no story, but the fact that they've managed to keep last night out of the papers must mean some very high up people don't *want* the story out there. But it doesn't mean they don't still want us; we're gonna have to get out of town for a bit.'

'We gotta git outta town, pardners!' Rob grinned, mimicking Terri in his worst cowboy accent.

'Can't you take *any*thing seriously, Rob?' Terri looked at him like she'd just smelled something bad. 'Dickhead.'

'Takes one to know one, sis.'

'Whatever.'

'Your trouble, sis?' Rob stood up, taking his jacket off the back of the chair. 'You take life too seriously, man.'

Paul watched him push his chair back in. 'Where you going?'

'Buggering off.' He nodded at Terri. 'Getting out, like she said. Wanna come?'

'What?' Paul frowned, like he hadn't quite heard what Rob had said.

'He's splitting . . . wants to know if you wanna go with him.'

'Me? What about you?'

'Doesn't look like I'm invited, right?' Terri stared at Rob, eyes narrowed.

'Rob?' Paul shifted uneasily in his chair.

'Shit-or-get-off-the-pot time, Pauly.' Rob was moving away, towards the café door, grinning. 'And believe me,' he nodded at Terri, 'you don't have a chance . . .'

Paul slowly sat back down, watching Rob turn and go out into the street, conflicting thoughts churning round in his head. Go with Rob – he could still catch him up – and see what the hell happened? Or . . . or what? He glanced over at Terri, sitting opposite him, and looked away, knowing Rob was right. He didn't have a cat's chance. But what was Rob doing, just walking out like that?

'Hey!' Terri snapped her fingers. 'Over here.'

Paul looked round. 'What?'

'You made the right decision . . . all he can do is steal cars. Without Sky and Orlando and the rest of us, without Omega Place, he's going to go off the rails. And you do not want to be there when he does.'

'So what're you gonna do?'

Terri stood up. 'Right now I have some stuff to fix, but I'll be back here, this café . . .' she checked the time on her mobile phone, '. . . in about three hours. Meet me just after six, OK?'

'Um . . . OK, yeah . . . but I've, like, got no . . .' Paul patted his jeans pockets.

'The bill's paid here.' Terri pushed some money across the table. 'Should keep you out of trouble till I'm back . . . don't spend it all at once.'

And then she was gone and he was on his own in the café again, only this time Rob wasn't in the bog, about to come back, and he didn't really reckon on the chances that Terri would be here in three hours' time. He couldn't believe she'd just walked out, too. No goodbye. Nothing.

Didn't even look back . . .

40

Monday 21st August, Thames House

Jane Mercer sat alone in her office. She felt deflated, some-how. Flat. The operation was over and she assumed the team would now be reassigned to other duties. From what she could gather people were talking, internally, in terms of the job having been successful, even taking into considera-tion the fact that two of theirs had been taken down. From her point of view she was just happy that, while not exactly covered in glory, she'd had a couple of appreciative emails. But what kind of riled her was that the action had been so effectively hushed up. Nothing in the papers, nothing on TV or the radio. Nothing about what had really occurred any-way. Like it had never happened.

She sighed, shaking her head at her own slightly ridicu-lous naivity. Grow up, girl. What did she expect – when did the truth, the whole truth and nothing but the truth ever apply to this place? On the desk in front of her was a large buff envelope, the type used for inter-office correspondence. It was from Markham and she supposed she ought to read it. Find out the verdict that really mattered.

Flicking up the rather old-fashioned metal fastener she took out the two files that were inside. A hand-written memo was paper-clipped to the top one. 'A difficult job well handled,' it said. 'Thought you might appreciate sight of the file I've sent to the Home Office. Please shred after reading.'

Momentarily nonplussed, Mercer picked up the first file and started reading.

INTERNAL MEMO – FOR YOUR EYES ONLY

FROM: Alex Markham, Director of Internal Affairs, MI5

TO: Michael Turner, PPS Home Secretary

Re: Omega Place

Michael,

The attached files comprise a full and detailed account of this department's operation last Saturday night/Sunday morning, and I thought a few bullet points might be of some help before you read the report in full.

- Henry Garden called me, at home, at about 1.50 a.m. Sunday morning. I taped the call, and a transcript is in the file. He'd obviously been drinking, and was rambling, but gave me a full and frank confession as to his recent conduct, implicating Nicholas Harvey, the owner and CEO of AquiLAN, the communications group, as the man blackmailing him, and the person ultimately behind Omega Place.

- Harvey is still in custody – we don't want him anywhere near a computer until the forensic accountants and investigators have finished going over everything in his offices with a fine-toothed comb. We have yet to decide what he should be charged with.

- Garden also implicated one Dean Mayhew, an ex-SAS soldier, whom he thought Harvey had hired. We

247

believe this is the man who was in the house when our people went in, and the person responsible for the two deaths and the injuries to our personnel. Unfortunately, Garden's information came too late for it to be of any use in changing the outcome of what happened.

- The Mayhew situation is in hand.
- This whole incident is being dressed up and given to the local media as a drugs bust, victims as yet unknown; considering the location, I don't think we'll have any difficulty at all in selling it as such and the story really doesn't have the legs to go national. We are, effectively, out of the picture, and have made the police first port of call for all information.
- The dead male, referred to originally as Orlando Welles, turns out to be aka James Hudson Baker, last known to us as a hard-left agitator in the late 80s, early 90s. He was, apparently, at university with Harvey, who was using him to run the Omega Place operation on the ground. Garden says that Harvey wanted Welles taken out of the equation, so to speak, because he wasn't obeying orders and his activities were gaining too much attention. Welles has no living relatives.
- The dead youth is assumed to be a Paul Hendry, but the three bullets Mayhew used to kill him (we still don't know why) completely destroyed any facial information that we might have used to ID him, as well as anything that could have constituted dental records. Using the drugs bust cover story, his parents are being informed today, and will have to make formal and final identification.

- The American, Jerome Petersen, is refusing to cooperate any further. He has been informed that his government has started extradition proceedings.
- The girl found with Baker, Isabel Morley, claims to have only been in the squat for a few days and to have no knowledge of what Baker, Petersen and the others were doing; as she appears in none of the photographic evidence we have, this is possibly true and it's likely we shall have to let her go, as her only crime is that of squatting.
- There are three remaining subjects at large – the female and two males who were photographed with Petersen in Bristol. We have no information as to who they might be. In his paperwork, Welles/Baker referred to people only by initials, so, by a process of elimination, we know that we are missing an RG, a TH and a TM. These three may well know about the RPA project, and as such I am advising that we should, in the short term, keep looking for them.

That about wraps it up. Bottom line, Omega Place has been closed down and I don't expect to hear any more about it, or its activities. And if anyone asks, no, we haven't found out why it was called by that name.

I gather the latest RPA night test flights, with the infra-red cameras, have been very successful – I hope to see one in action myself in the next few weeks.

Yours etc.,

Alex

Mercer closed the file, put it on her desk and picked up the other one. What was her bottom line going to be?

INTERNAL MEMO – FOR YOUR EYES ONLY

FROM: Alex Markham, Director of Internal Affairs, MI5

TO: Jane Mercer

Re: Omega Place

Jane,

Just a short note to thank you and your team for the sterling work put in on this operation, which is now effectively closed down. I know you may find yourself at odds with the facts – what with Dean Mayhew and three of the Omega Place people unaccounted for – but as you will have seen from the Home Office file, there is still work to be done in this regard and I am just waiting on confirmation that it can go ahead.

I would therefore like to keep your team together for the foreseeable future. I have a twenty-minute window at 5.00 p.m. today and would like to brief you then.

Alex

41

Monday 21st August, King's Cross

Paul had got back to the café with about a quarter of an hour to spare. About three hours, just like Terri had said. Fifteen minutes and one cup of tepid coffee later, it was just after six and there was still no sign of her. He went back to looking through a copy of the *Daily Mail* someone had left at the table, idly scanning the pages, not really taking in what he was reading. '*BURGLARY GOES WRONG – ENDS IN MURDER*' . . . the headline caught his eye and he started reading properly.

Some bloke, a successful insurance broker living in a place called Hendon had apparently surprised a burglar in his house the night before and ended up getting shot for his trouble; he was an OK type, apparently, at least according to a neighbour the journalist had talked to. The story ended with a paragraph detailing how much gun crime had risen in the UK over the last twelve months. It pissed Paul off that some businessman deserved a half-page story in the papers when he got shot and killed, but Tommy and Orlando didn't. Even when you were dead, money made a difference. Without it, you weren't worth anything.

'Hi.'

Paul looked up. Some girl, dark hair, cut short, wearing smart, kind of office clothes, was pulling out a chair and sitting opposite him.

'Yeah . . .?'

'What d'you think?'

It was the voice. 'Terri? What . . . ?'

'They're looking for a blonde, with long hair, jeans and stuff, so . . . ta-da!' Terri spread out both her hands.

She looked, not only completely different, but, if anything, even more unattainable; all Paul could do was nod and wonder how she'd managed to afford to do everything . . . the hair, the clothes . . .

'Like the look?'

'Very nice, Terri.' Paul knew now, beyond any shadow of a doubt that, like Rob had said, he hadn't a chance in hell. 'So did you just come back to, like, say goodbye? You didn't have to, you could've walked out, like Rob. I'd've understood.'

'No, Pauly, I wanted to say goodbye. Leave you thinking good things about me.' she smiled. 'You never know, we might meet again somewhere.'

'Yeah, right . . .'

'Never say never. And I got you something . . .' Terri put a large black leather bag, another new purchase, on the table and began taking stuff out as she looked for something. 'Here it is.'

Paul looked at the envelope she was holding out for him to take. 'What is it?'

'Take a look.'

He tore the pristine white paper. Money, and what looked like a train ticket. He looked questioningly at Terri.

'It's an open ticket to Newcastle, plus a bit.' She stood up and began putting everything back in her bag. 'Better than hitching, right?'

'How d'you know I want to go back?'

'Because you hadn't left home for good, because you

should go back and see if you really want to leave.' Terri hitched her bag on to her shoulder and came round the table. 'Bye, Pauly. Have the best life you can.'

Before Paul could say thanks, Terri was threading her way through the tables and was gone. Which meant he was alone again. Properly alone this time, as there was no one to come back now. He looked in the envelope again, counting a couple of hundred quid in twenties. Where the hell had all that come from? What had she done, gone and robbed a flaming bank or what? Which was when he noticed the piece of paper Terri had left behind on the table by mistake.

He picked it up, a receipt from some shop. Made out to someone called Teresa Hyde-Barrett. Was that who Terri Hyde really was? Some double-barrelled girl who'd been slumming it for a bit of excitement? And now that it was getting too exciting she was going back. So maybe Sky had been wrong about that. Maybe, with enough money, you could go back. Lucky her, then, if she could simply turn herself into someone else so easily . . . unlike him. He didn't exist any more. He was nobody now. How was he going to start a new life – that wasn't going to happen with a train ticket and a couple of hundred quid. And was Terri right, that he'd not really left home for good? If he hadn't, how could a dead boy ever go home?

Paul took his mobile out of Tommy's jacket pocket. Truth was, he'd never thought it through, leaving home; he'd slammed the door of the house shut, but hadn't locked it or thrown away the key. He could call home, talk to his mum. She wouldn't know anything about what had happened . . .

He sat bolt upright in the chair, shocked rigid by what he'd just thought. *No one knew about what had happened.*

If the cops really were covering it all up, no one out in the big, wide world knew anything about the shooting, that Paul Hendry was supposed to be dead. Not even his mum.

He sat, completely stunned. Confused, tired and strung out by everything that he'd been through, he couldn't seem to make his brain function properly. If it wasn't in the papers, then, surely, it hadn't been on TV or anything. And if that was true, no one knew about it – and if *that* was an actual fact, then it hadn't happened. That was logical, wasn't it? Like Orlando always said, history was always written by those with the power. Nothing was real, and there was no such thing as truth . . .

Paul picked up his phone and dialled his mum's mobile, only remembering, when the answering service picked up, that she never liked taking calls from numbers she didn't know, and she wouldn't know the number he was using now, the one Tommy, poor dead Tommy, had given him. One of her little things, that. He cut the call, not leaving a message.

Staring at the screen of his phone, he wondered what his mum would say when she heard his voice. She'd be totally hacked off with him, probably, but glad, too. Happy he'd phoned. He punched in the digits for the house phone and pressed 'call'. Maybe a dead boy could go back home, after all . . .